MANNEQUIN AND WIFE

Yellow Shoe Fiction
Michael Griffith, Series Editor

MANNEQUIN AND WIFE

— STORIES —

JEN FAWKES

LOUISIANA STATE UNIVERSITY PRESS
BATON ROUGE

Published by Louisiana State University Press
www.lsupress.org

Designer: Laura Roubique Gleason
Typeface: MillerText

Library of Congress Cataloging-in-Publication Data
Names: Fawkes, Jen, author.
Title: Mannequin and wife : stories / Jen Fawkes.
Description: Baton Rouge : Louisiana State University Press, [2020] | Series: Yellow shoe fiction
Identifiers: LCCN 2020005556 (print) | LCCN 2020005557 (ebook) | ISBN 978-0-8071-7391-6 (paperback ; alk. paper) | ISBN 978-0-8071-7413-5 (pdf) | ISBN 978-0-8071-7414-2 (epub)
Classification: LCC PS3606.A945 A6 2020 (print) | LCC PS3606.A945 (ebook) | DDC 813/.6—dc23
LC record available at https://lccn.loc.gov/2020005556
LC ebook record available at https://lccn.loc.gov/2020005557

To my one and only sister, Anna Terry Fawkes
(1972–1991)

Indeed, one's attachment to a man depends largely on the elegance of his leave-taking. When he jumps out of bed, scurries about the room, tightly fastens his trouser-sash, rolls up the sleeves of his Court cloak, over-robe, or hunting costume, stuffs his belongings into the breast of his robe and then briskly secures the outer sash—one really begins to hate him.

—Sei Shonagon, "Hateful Things"

There is no excellent beauty that hath not some strangeness in the proportion.

—Francis Bacon, "Of Beauty"

Contents

MANNEQUIN AND WIFE

Sometimes, They Kill Each Other

We're worried about Misty. The youngest stenographer in the pool, she's been with the firm less than three months. Like the rest of us, she graduated from Ms. Purdy's Academy, the finest stenography school in the tri-state area, and like Penny, the most senior of us, and Phyllis and Mabel, identical twins who work in tandem, Misty took top honors in her class. It isn't her typing or her shorthand that has us biting our manicured nails and tugging nervously on the collars of our cashmere sweaters. It's her flagrant flouting of convention.

Each of us took an instant liking to Misty, from Holly, who can be an utter grump, to Janine, who's recently switched to decaf, to Penny, who can take months to warm up to a new girl. Having come from Ms. Purdy's, Misty fit into our tight-knit-sweater-set-and-sensible-shoe collective nicely. The fact that her bangs were a bit short and her lipstick the wrong shade of pink didn't bother us in the least—such imperfections made Misty more appealing. After gently correcting her mistakes, we felt a motherly sense of accomplishment, as though we'd had a hand in her development.

At eight a.m., we stenographers hit the ground running. We don't stop until the other side of six p.m. There's no nesting for us; unlike secretaries, we lack the luxury of a desk. Ours is a transient, hardscrabble existence, one that finds us perched on a chair in Personnel in the morning and, after an egg salad or turkey or ham on rye from the sandwich cart, wolfed in the elevator, trotting through the halls after a roaming, dictating vice president in the afternoon. With nothing but a notebook, two pencils, and a thermos full of strong black coffee (or decaf, in the case of Janine), we go where the wind blows us.

Misty was only two weeks out of Ms. Purdy's and adjusting nicely to the demands of the steno pool when into the bullpen slid a memo announcing an interoffice duel. The walls of the bullpen, a narrow first-floor room in which we type up dictation or pace restlessly, ready to sprint to the elevator banks at a moment's notice, are painted the color of strained peas. The desks sag, the carpet is worn, and on the west wall hangs a framed poster of a long-haired kitten clinging to a tree branch. "HANG IN THERE!" blazes in red letters across its stretched, exposed belly.

"Memo!" Penny cried, waving the sheet of paper above her graying brown bun. "Ladies! We have a memo!"

As stenographers, we receive few memorandums, and the appearance of one meant something momentous was afoot. We dropped nail files and compacts and glossy magazines and flocked around our senior sister.

"Oh my!" she exclaimed, her eyes gleaming. "It looks like Mr. Venable's challenged one of the junior executives."

The door of the bullpen opened and in marched Misty, who'd been taking dictation on the twelfth floor. Our fists unclenched; our tongues retreated into our mouths as we turned our collective gaze on the youngest and most innocent among us.

"What's going on?" she asked.

"We've had a memo." Penny stepped forward. "I'm afraid there's going to be a duel, dear."

Interoffice duels are a frequent occurrence. Any actual or

perceived insult to an executive by another is grounds for a challenge: stealing another man's lunch, sabotaging his presentation, flirting with his secretary, stabbing him in the back, giving him a weak handshake or a funny look. Notoriously sensitive, executives believe the only way to restore their honor is to demonstrate their willingness to die for it. They gain satisfaction at twenty paces in the courtyard of the firm's high-rise, using a pair of dueling pistols the CEO keeps under lock and key.

In the bullpen, we watched Misty's pearl-pink lower lip quiver, each of us thinking of her own first duel. Fresh from Ms. Purdy's, we stenographers arrived at the firm artless as infants. The first time we saw a man slain over a trifle, we were horror-stricken. The next time, too. But after months, then years, of dealing with executives, we found that though some are lascivious and some misogynistic, all executives see us as one interchangeable automaton put on earth for the sole purpose of taking their dictation. And we became accustomed to watching them off one another. Duels shattered the monotony of our days, and we started looking forward to them with fluttery stomachs, with a sickening intensity, with a morbidity of which we were ashamed, of which we never spoke.

"There, now," Penny said, wiping tears from Misty's cheeks. "It's not so bad. Holly, get her a cup of tea, will you?"

Grumbling, Holly stalked toward the break room.

"When?" Misty sniffed, as Penny settled her into a chair.

"Friday at noon. Mr. Venable's challenged a junior executive. A Mr. Fisk."

Misty groaned.

"What is it, dear?"

"I was just in Mr. Fisk's office! He shared his Danish with me. He was such a nice man!" With that, Misty's face dissolved.

Penny held her until she was called away to take a letter for an account manager on fifteen. One by one we comforted Misty, wiping away her tears, until in turn we too were forced to abandon our sister and race to the aid of an impatient executive.

Friday dawned crisp and clear, and we stenographers traveled by train or bus or bicycle or automobile to the firm, our thoughts bent on the impending duel. On duel days, the normally neutral air of the high-rise crackles. Everyone—from the greenest boy in the basement mail room to the vice presidents on nineteen—bounces through the halls, jingling pocket change and whistling off-key tunes. People who never look up from the gray carpet cry "Good morning!" with a nod and a wink for whoever is listening. Smiles and handshakes abound. Pats on the back long overdue are meted out. People give each other impromptu massages. Executives and accountants wear their brightest neckties. Secretaries show off even more leg than usual.

Misty, who lived less than a mile from the high-rise, was late. We paced the bullpen, biting our nails and glancing at the clock. At 8:15, when she wandered through the door like a bewildered lamb, the poor dear was shaking, and we pressed around her in a tight ring of sisterly support.

"You'll be all right," said Penny.

"It'll be over before you know it," said Janine with a decaffeinated yawn.

"You can always cover your eyes the first time. We did," said Phyllis and Mabel.

"Hrrmp," grumbled Holly.

On duel days little work is done, so few of us were called away in the morning, and before we knew it, noon was upon us.

We joined the flow of employees crowding the halls, all wriggling toward the same destination like spawning salmon. With linked arms, we allowed the crush to sweep us into the courtyard, then fought to hold a position less than twenty feet from the action.

In an area roped off with yellow caution tape stood Mr. Venable and Mr. Fisk. Mr. Venable, who'd been with the firm twenty-five years, was an old hand at dueling. He'd challenged and dispatched more executives than all the rest put together. He was the reason, it was said, that executives at the firm were on the whole so young—he'd killed off an entire generation. Any insult would prompt a challenge from Mr. Venable, and he was an expert marksman. No one went so far as to say he took pleasure in killing, but we in the bullpen had our suspicions. Once, when Mr. Venable had mumbled while Janine was taking a letter, she'd asked him to repeat himself and he'd leapt to his feet and drawn back his big fist. His nostrils flared to the size of nickels as he towered over her, shaking.

"I swear to God," she'd later said of the incident, "there was murder in his eyes."

Whether Mr. Venable would have taken a life outside the confines of a sanctioned duel was unclear, but everyone at the firm knew not to cross him. We all had to wonder what Mr. Fisk had done to call down his rage.

"Look at him," said Misty, who sagged between Phyllis and Mabel. "Doesn't he look nice?"

Mr. Fisk did look nice. He was tall and wore wire-rimmed glasses. His light brown hair was just beginning to pull away from his temples. He stood very straight, with his back to Mr. Venable, who was doing deep knee bends and grunting. Both men had removed their suit jackets and rolled up their shirtsleeves. Neither had loosened his tie. Mr. Fisk kept glancing at the pistol in his right hand as though he was surprised to find it there.

"Do you know what he told me?" Misty said. "When I was in his office?"

"What, dear?" asked Penny.

"That he'd made his final student loan payment that morning. He was so happy!" Misty buried her face in her hands. Wrapping their arms around her, Phyllis and Mabel cooed into her ears.

Excited voices rose from the churning crush of employees that filled the courtyard. We stenographers had snagged a prime spot. To our right, the boys from Accounting held an equally advantageous position. Directly behind us were the people from Personnel, and across the courtyard the secretaries had winked and flirted their way up front. They stood pressed against the tape that cordoned off the dueling zone, while behind them executives milled around in a section reserved for their use. A girl with a tray of drinks and snacks circulated among them. Three beach balls floated through the air. Whenever one came anywhere near Holly, she punched it with a satisfied grunt.

Janine yawned. "Isn't it about time to get this thing started?"

The CEO blew his tin whistle. A hush fell. The forgotten beach balls bounced to the concrete. Misters Venable and Fisk stood back-to-back in the middle of the courtyard. Each man held his pistol in front of his face, its barrel pointed up into the cloudless blue sky. When the CEO blew his whistle again, the two executives stepped forward.

Our nails dug into our palms. Our stomachs fluttered. Our knees trembled. Twenty paces was the standard, and along with the rest of the crowd, we all counted under our breath. All, that is, except Misty. Seemingly oblivious to the proceedings, she studied her brown oxfords. She clasped her hands in a tight knot at her waist.

At twelve paces, at fifteen, we strained forward. We felt the hot breath of those behind us on our necks.

At eighteen paces, at nineteen, our tightened muscles quaked.

At twenty paces, Misters Venable and Fisk spun. They aimed. They fired. They fell.

A single scream sounded, one that pierced the crowd's paralysis. It was Misty. Her pearl-pink lips hung open. Paramedics rushed to the fallen executives as we speculated in feverish whispers.

"Both men down!" said Penny. "This hasn't happened since Mr. Gibson challenged Mr. Beavers!"

"Has Mr. Venable been hit before?" asked Janine.

"He was grazed once, but he refused to go home. Just wound his handkerchief around his arm and worked through the afternoon."

Holly jerked her head toward Misty, who hadn't moved. She hadn't blinked.

"At least he got a piece of Mr. Venable, your Mr. Fisk," said Phyllis and Mabel. "Misty?" The twins waved their manicured fingers in front of her eyes, but Misty didn't respond.

The crowd released a collective sigh, and we looked up to see Mr. Venable rising to his feet. The paramedics had removed his shirt, and he stood between them, an oxygen mask covering his face, blood flowing from a hole in his right shoulder. Slowly, he lifted his right hand as high as his waist. He wiggled the fingers. Behind the oxygen mask, he seemed to be smiling.

"Where's Misty?" asked Penny.

We spotted our youngest sister ducking under the caution tape and into the dueling zone. Mr. Fisk was sprawled on the concrete, his glasses gone, his shirt open, his fingers still clutching the pistol, red pooling around him. The paramedics who'd been pumping his perforated chest and breathing into his mouth stood. They turned to the crowd and shook their heads. Misty threw herself on top of his body. One of the paramedics pulled her away. She was smiling. Blood streaked her face, her hands, her ivory sweater set. It was on her teeth. We stenographers shook our heads. We knew that even if she used Woolite, that sweater set would never be the same.

On Monday morning, Misty walked into the bullpen wearing gray sweats and tennis shoes. Her hair was pulled into a lopsided blond ponytail. Her eyes were swollen and red. Without pearl-pink lipstick, her face looked naked.

From where we sat and stood sipping coffee and tea from white Styrofoam, gossiping about the secretaries and flipping through fashion magazines and proofreading typed copy and filing our nails, we shuddered. The vague fear that gripped us at the sight of Misty couldn't fit into words. We were like rabbits sensing the imminent destruction of our warren before a bulldozer has even been secured.

After Misty was called up to the fourteenth floor, Penny touched her tight, graying brown bun. "The poor dear's in shock," she said. "Don't worry. She'll come around."

We nodded. We wanted so badly to believe her.

In the coming days, however, we were forced to admit that the change in Misty was more lasting. She slunk through the halls like a thief. Meeting her in the elevator or the ladies' room became unsettling, and it wasn't just her slovenly appearance—she seemed to have forgotten how to chitchat. The things that concerned us no longer interested her, and we started using the mirrors in our compacts to look for her around corners. At the sight of her dejected figure approaching, we would duck into a broom closet or copy room until she'd passed.

In the bullpen, she was quiet and withdrawn. She clacked the keys of a typewriter at ninety words a minute or sat staring into space. We tried to include her in conversation, to reach beyond her downtrodden facade and draw out the girl we'd been so impressed by, the sister who'd fit so nicely into our collective.

"What do you think, Misty?" asked Janine, who was making new drapes for her apartment. "Roses or peacocks?"

Misty couldn't be bothered to lift her eyes from the worn carpet. She couldn't be bothered to shrug. "I don't see how it matters."

Janine stomped off in a huff. As the rest of us tried to calm her, Penny knelt beside Misty. It was tough love time.

"Look, dear," she said, "we were all upset by our first duel. But you're behaving like a spoiled child."

Misty blinked rapidly.

"I know it's hard to believe, but it gets easier. It really does."

Misty did not look convinced.

"Is this about Mr. Fisk? I know you thought he was a nice man, but had he lived, I guarantee the next time he saw you he wouldn't have known you from Phyllis or Mabel. Executives aren't like us, dear. They have no compassion. They're cold and self-involved, and sometimes, they kill each other."

Misty mumbled something about being needed on floor fifteen and fled. Collectively, we watched her go. Collectively, we sighed.

"You really think she'll come around, Penny?" asked Phyllis and Mabel.

Under the bullpen fluorescents, Penny looked tired. Her bun seemed more gray than brown. "I don't know, ladies." She shook her head. "I honestly don't know."

"Hrrmp," grumbled Holly.

To our relief, Misty did come around. She ditched the sweats, but sensible shoes and sweater sets did not take their place. Instead, she took to wearing slip dresses and precariously high heels. Her blond hair, loosed from its lopsided ponytail, flowed down her back. Her pearl-pink lipstick was replaced by a deep shade of crimson.

"Let's not criticize," Penny said to the rest of us. "At least she's shaving her legs."

Two weeks after he dispatched Mr. Fisk, Mr. Venable returned to work. He'd spent five days in the hospital, and his right arm was bound to his chest. The secretaries of the nineteenth floor strung up a *WELCOME BACK, MR. V!* banner and invited the entire firm to a lunchtime party featuring miniature quiches, miniature ham sandwiches, miniature cupcakes, and fruit punch. At noon, we stenographers lifted paper cups to toast Mr. Venable, who stood in his office doorway looking bored. We snuck nervous glances at Misty, but if she was still upset about Mr. Fisk she didn't show it. Our youngest sister may have started dressing like a slut, but she was still one of us, and we were proud of how well she was handling the situation. As the party wore on, Misty approached Mr. Venable, and before we knew it they were chatting like old friends.

"I knew she'd come around." Penny's lips, like the lips of

every employee at the party, were stained fruit punch red. "She just needed time."

"Look at them." Janine peeled the pink paper from a miniature chocolate cupcake. "What could they possibly be talking about?"

Phyllis and Mabel guessed that they were discussing movies. Holly made an off-color comment, something only she could get away with, which made the rest of us blush and giggle. When we looked again at Mr. Venable's office, the door was closed, and he and Misty were nowhere to be seen.

Over the next month, three executives issued challenges, and to our surprise Misty was front and center for each interoffice duel. A far cry from the girl who'd sagged between Phyllis and Mabel as Misters Venable and Fisk stepped across the courtyard, turned, and fired, she now pressed anxiously into the caution tape, cheering and whistling. Truth be told, her enthusiasm struck the rest of us as over-the-top. We stenographers have always been careful to hide the excitement dueling inspires in us. Bloodlust, in our opinion, is not very becoming. On duel days, we started distancing ourselves from Misty. We were alarmed by her behavior, and it affected our mood. We sniped at one another for no reason. Phyllis and Mabel argued for the first time since high school. We found ourselves no longer able to fully appreciate the sight of a dead executive.

Misty spent less and less time in the bullpen. We spotted her in the halls, chatting with secretaries and accountants. At times, coming around a corner, we caught sight of her tumbling yellow hair and did not recognize her. It was a shock to realize she was our youngest sister, a member of our tight-knit collective—one of us. Misty's actions felt traitorous, and we started censoring ourselves around her. We no longer had any idea what she was thinking. We felt her drifting, and a part of us wanted to bring her back into the fold while another part wanted to cut her loose.

"I've been with the firm thirty years." Penny spoke in tremulous tones. With the exception of Misty, who was taking dictation on nineteen, and Holly, who stood guard at the door, we ringed our senior sister in the bullpen. "Stenographers have never mixed with secretaries or accountants."

"I can't believe she took top honors at Ms. Purdy's," sniffed Phyllis and Mabel.

"Her behavior on duel days is absolutely ghoulish," said Janine.

"I've never been wrong about a hire," Penny said, swaying on her feet. Phyllis and Mabel rolled an office chair over and she collapsed into it. "Every one of my girls has fit into the pool perfectly."

"It's not your fault." Janine patted Penny's shoulder. "It's Misty. I hate to say it, but she just doesn't belong."

The air was tense. We couldn't look one another in the eye. We'd taken Misty under our collective wing, and we were all responsible. Whatever was wrong with her was also wrong with us.

"What do we do?" said Phyllis and Mabel in small voices.

"What can we do?" Penny wrapped her arms around herself. She shivered. Her bun was coming loose and gray hairs floated around her head. "We try to make her come around. She's one of us. We can't just turn our backs."

Poor Penny has gone home for the afternoon—her first sick day in ten years. Holly, Phyllis, and Mabel have been elected to do the talking when Misty returns. Holly because she is direct and takes no nonsense, and Phyllis and Mabel for their ability to soften the blows. As, pacing and biting our manicured nails, we await her, we each consider what it would be like to be in Misty's shoes, to walk into the bullpen and find our sisters waiting to ambush us with a talk about how our behavior is affecting the pool, about how that behavior must stop.

At the sound of a commotion in the lobby, we open the bullpen door and file out. There, in front of the reception desk, is Mr. Venable. His hands are cuffed behind his back. Two police officers drag him from the high-rise.

"What's going on?" Janine asks the receptionist, who has fled her desk and cowers in a corner.

"Mr. Venable killed a junior executive, a Mr. Cooper! He killed him in cold blood!"

It seems as though the question of whether Mr. Venable would commit murder has been answered, but we cannot help wondering why he would do so when, by challenging Mr. Cooper to a duel, he could kill him with impunity.

"He shot him with the dueling pistols!" the receptionist continues. "A stenographer discovered Mr. Cooper's body! The CEO searched the executive offices and found the pistols in Mr. Venable's desk!"

We turn to the elevator banks as a set of doors slides open and Misty appears, framed in the rectangular box. She wears a white dress and red high-heeled sandals. Secretaries and boys from the mail room and people from Personnel crowd around and ply her with questions about Mr. Cooper's body, as though they've never witnessed an interoffice duel. As though they think murder and sanctioned killing leave two entirely different kinds of corpses.

Misty is holding up well, considering, and as the police take her downtown to make a statement, we stenographers retire to the bullpen. We sit at desks, flipping the pages of magazines and drinking coffee and filing our nails and typing, but something has changed. A shred of collective knowledge has disturbed our minds. We share a vision of Misty firing the dueling pistols, unloading their contents into Mr. Cooper's chest. The poor man's mouth falls open. He thrusts out his hands as though they can protect him.

Casting sideways glances at one another, we wonder about the members of our tight-knit group. What is hidden in Holly's heart? What lurks in the corners of Janine's consciousness? Has Phyllis ever gotten really angry at Mabel? Angry enough to kill? We cannot plumb the depths of our sweater-set-and-sensible-shoe-wearing sisters, and we are filled with dread. We are filled with doubt.

It is after five o'clock when a hand rattles the doorknob. We know it is Misty. Our instinct is to herd together, but our belief in the safety of numbers has shattered. Each and every one of us can think only of herself.

Separately, we rise to our feet.

We Can Learn from the Sawhorse

Her girls are chasing a goat around a petting zoo when Pearl recalls Stan and Ollie standing stiff-legged in the listing, oil-stained garage of her childhood, a stoic pair trotted out only when Hank decided to build something that required support. Otherwise, they were Pearl's: more than pets, more than friends. Companions. She sneaked them lumps of sugar and the rare carrot, and when Hank was gone or unconscious, she climbed atop first Ollie, then Stan, and galloped through fields of wheat or woolly jungles or along distant shorelines with pounding surf. She gifted them heads, manes, tails. Saddles. Perfectly swayed backs. Ollie was a piebald; Stan was jet black with a star-shaped blaze between his soft eyes. Then one afternoon Hank caught Pearl astride Stan, cantering round a course, jumping box hedges and water hazards. He ordered her down, but she refused. He rummaged in shelves and cubbies, found his felling hatchet, and as she watched, paralyzed, her father hacked Ollie to sticks. *Get down,* he growled, but she wouldn't. She clung to Stan's wooden spine, limbs wrapped tight, shielding him. Eventually, Hank shrugged. *Stupid kid,* he laughed. *It's a goddamned two-by-four.* Once he'd jumped into his pickup and peeled out of the drive, calling up a funnel of dust, Pearl climbed down. Gathered the remains of Ollie, hauled them outside, dropped them in the patchy grass. She attempted to reassemble Ollie, but his pieces wouldn't fit. The parts no longer made a whole. So she rose. Reentered the garage. Grasped her father's hatchet and stood over Stan. *Hold still, boy,* she said, tears leaking, hefting the blade above her head. *This is going to hurt me more than it does you.* She carried the remains of Stan outside, mixed them with the splintered pieces that had once been Ollie, and went to work. The wood seemed to know what Pearl wanted before she did, to come together of its own free will. Two hours later, she stepped back. Though it was secured with neither nails nor glue, screws nor twine, her new creature was solid. Sturdy. Enormous. Rearing up on hind legs. Slashing at the pinking sky. Roaring, teeth agleam in slanted light. Pearl circled her creation, stroked its flanks, and a thrill raced through her. She clambered up and settled in the crook of its shoulder, facing the drive, where Hank's truck would eventually reappear. Whatever happened—if her father backhanded her or choked her unconscious or set fire to what she'd made—she knew she'd be OK. Hank could build things, and smash them, but he didn't have Pearl's gifts. *I can make things live,* she whispered as darkness cloaked the scene, as streetlamps flickered on, as headlights swept the mangy yard, as her Companion breathed evenly, lovingly, beneath her. *I can make things live.*

Come Back, Rita

Mickey's been on Percocet three months; he's been on the case one hour; he's been a PI twenty-nine years. She answers the door in a pair of lavender stretch pants and a patterned silk blouse that transports him instantly to the shore. Mickey sees waves. Spurts of foam. Or does he see scales? It's all blues, greens, purples. Not unlike a bruise, a fading shiner. In any case, the blouse is shimmering. It's winking at him. She's holding still, but the blouse is in motion. Her silvering hair is bobbed, neatly. Tucked behind one pierced ear. She wears pearl earrings; her feet are bare and quite beautiful; she says her name is Naomi.

"You're Mr. Mercer?"

"I am."

She touches a gold locket suspended from her neck. Smiles. "Won't you come in?"

The blouse is long, but it doesn't cover her ass, which is quite firm for a woman of her age. She probably does yoga. Mickey studies its motion as they move over dense carpeting into one of those showplace living rooms. The kind that's only ever seen by company or the cleaning lady, full of breakable and sentimental things. There's a glass-topped coffee table; a sectional sofa stands sentry around the room's perimeter; impressive intact seashells, ceramic figurines, and framed photos are positioned on every surface. Mickey hands Naomi his hat and coat and settles on the sofa's sea-foam cushions, clearing his throat over what sounds exactly like a rushing tide.

"Mrs. Stein . . ."

"Naomi."

"Naomi," Mickey says, flipping open the small notebook he's retrieved from his trouser pocket, "how long has your husband been missing?"

"My husband?" She's not far from him, sitting cross-legged on a piece of sectional, her pretty feet tucked under her firm glutes. Mickey can smell expensive laundry detergent, lavender soap, deodorant, brine. He thinks of Rita, of summers they spent in the Keys, of chasing her along the shore, how their footprints were erased almost instantly, how cold the skin of her breasts was once he'd freed those pretty white orbs from the prison of her bathing suit top, how the gritty sand that collected beneath the stretch fabric always got in his mouth. The wonder of fucking his own wife in freshly laundered rental beds.

"Yes," he says, squinting at a page in his notebook. Thirty minutes before Mickey took Naomi's call, the .38 Special bullet nestled against his twelfth thoracic vertebra started causing him severe discomfort, so he popped a second Percocet, and he's now unable to interpret his own scrawl. "Frederick?" he says. "Or Felix? Fabian? Ferdinand?"

"Frank," Naomi says. "My husband's name is Frank."

Mickey studies the notebook. He turns it upside down. For the first time in his life, he cannot decipher what he himself has written, and he feels like some dim-witted monster. He closes the cover, returns the notebook to his pocket. "Frank," he says. "Right. Sorry."

"Not a problem."

"When did you last see Frank?"

Naomi smiles, unfolds her legs, places her feet on the carpet, sits up straight. She's as polished as a set of wedding silver. Everything about the woman screams *privilege.* She couldn't be less like Rita, who came from the wrong side of the wrong side of the tracks. Rita's abusive parents—traveling-sideshow faith healers—dragged Rita and her eight siblings all over the southeastern U.S. before settling down in a rusting Central Florida double-wide. Mickey's family wasn't wealthy, but his parents nearly disowned him for eloping with a girl from the trailer park.

"Two days ago," Naomi says, "around noon. Perhaps a little earlier."

"So Frank's been missing more than forty-eight hours."

Naomi shakes her head. "Mr. Mercer," she says, "it's not my husband who's missing."

"It's not?"

She shakes her head again.

"He's here then?"

"No."

The living room of the two-story Spanish Colonial Revival is not unlike a terrarium. Sunlight streams in through three floor-to-ceiling windows. Mickey feels oppressed by the glare. His head begins to pulse and he places a hand over his brow, rubs his temples the way Rita once did. They hadn't been married a month when Mickey realized that his wife possessed a paranormal knowledge of human anatomy. Whenever he hurt, Rita knew innately which part of him she should press, knead, or stroke to provide relief. After massage therapy school, Rita opened a practice out of their home and business boomed. She attempted to teach Mickey the things she knew about manipulating muscle and connective tissue, but Mickey never could hold a candle to his wife. He still misses her touch.

"So you haven't seen Frank," Mickey says, "for more than forty-eight hours, but you don't think he's missing."

Naomi nods.

"Do you know where he is?"

"I do," she says. "Well, I know what he's doing, anyway."

Rita used to tell people the same thing whenever Mickey was on a three-day stakeout, running down some cheating husband or disability scammer or crooked accountant.

"Mrs. Stein . . ."

"Naomi."

"Naomi, I thought you wanted me to find your husband."

"But he's not missing."

"Where is he then?" says Mickey. "Where is Frank?"

Naomi stands, advances on Mickey so swiftly he recoils. Her toenails, painted lavender, now butt up against his brogans. Naomi bends at the waist; he feels her breath on his cheek; he realizes he's getting an erection.

"My husband," she says softly, "is out chasing his monster."

Mickey holds himself very still. He wonders if this is a euphemism with which he's unfamiliar. Naomi's eyes are light brown, almost golden. On the surface, they're nothing like Rita's, which were bright blue. Like the sky after all-night thunderstorms. It was storming when Mickey last saw his wife, kneeling over him on their front hall floorboards, the Colt Detective Special he'd given her for protection in her right hand, those blue eyes hidden in shadow.

"What's wrong with me?" Naomi says, tucking her hair behind both ears. "I haven't offered you a thing. Would you like some coffee, Mr. Mercer? Or a cup of tea?"

Drinking coffee after noon keeps Mickey up all night, so he takes tea. White jasmine. Naomi joins him. When he asks how long she and Frank have been in the house, she says three years. Says they moved to Tampa from San Francisco.

"Traded one Bay Area for another," Mickey says.

Naomi nods. "My whole family's on the West Coast. We only

came here for Frank's work. Tampa's the Lightning Capital of North America, you know."

"What does Frank do?"

Naomi sips her tea, replaces the cup in its saucer. She looks at Mickey quizzically. "He's a mad scientist."

Mickey waits for her to laugh. She doesn't.

"Mad scientist," he says. "I thought they only had those in the movies."

Naomi shakes her head.

"So when you said," Mickey says, "that your husband is out chasing his monster . . ."

"I meant," she says, "that Frank's spent the last six months in his basement lab, constructing a pseudohuman out of body parts he's stolen from cemeteries and morgues. Four nights ago, during that record-breaking cloud-to-ground lightning storm, he managed to harness electromagnetic impulses and channel them into his creation, bringing it to life. Two days ago, his creature broke free of its restraints. It tore the basement door off its hinges, staggered through the garden, and vanished into that cypress stand out back. When Frank got home from the farmers market, I told him what happened. He took off after his monster, and I haven't seen him since."

For what seems a century, Mickey tries to come up with a response. He sips his tea; he wonders if this privileged, polished housewife actually believes what she's telling him; he keeps thinking about kissing her exquisite instep. The glaring light outside the floor-to-ceiling windows is softening. Withering. The day is dying.

"Well, Mr. Mercer?" Naomi finally says.

"Mickey."

"Mickey," she says, "do you think you can help me?"

Mickey never wanted to cheat on Rita. But he did. Multiple times. With women like Naomi. Clean, pleasantly scented housewives. Pretty women with tender hearts and good intentions. Women with manicured nails and toned triceps. Women whose husbands had gone out for a pouch of pipe tobacco or a pesto and arugula pizza and never come back. Women who'd really done nothing wrong. Women who deserved to be treated gingerly. Mickey always showered before he came home to Rita. He always stood, for quite a long time, before the front door, studying the peephole, wondering if his wife knew. If she would feel the afterglow of adultery in his muscles. If he would find Rita in the hall, waiting.

"Yes," Mickey says. He stands and crosses to Naomi, who sits opposite him on the sectional. As he settles beside her he takes one of her hands, and the sound of the rushing sea rises in volume, drowning out his thoughts. "I think I can help. The first thing I'll need is a glass of water."

After he pops another Percocet, Mickey retrieves the notebook from his pocket. He asks Naomi where she imagines her husband's monster might have gone. She answers without hesitation.

"The beach."

Mickey writes the word *Beach.* "Why would it go there?"

Naomi shrugs. "Who doesn't like the beach?"

Mickey drives the BMW convertible parked in the Steins' redbrick driveway. He and Naomi find Cypress Point Park, Davis Islands Beach, and the Ben T. Davis Beach deserted. They sit in the car in the Ben T. Davis Beach parking lot, watching the sun lower itself into the sea.

"I don't understand," Naomi says, shaking her head. "I felt so certain."

"Maybe Frank's monster went to Clearwater," Mickey says. "Or Saint Pete."

As they make their way back to her neighborhood, Naomi tells Mickey that she and Frank have been married thirty-one years. They met at a house party in Pasadena. Frank was at Caltech, studying biochemistry, neurobiology, and biomechanics. Naomi was in her first year at the ArtCenter College of Design. The couple spent the entire night moving from room to room, surrounded by people but ignoring them, talking about the human body, its design, and possible ways to improve it; life on other planets; the stories of Philip K. Dick. The rising sun found Naomi and Frank on a sofa some fun-loving students had parked atop a pool table, holding hands, a strange young man with an Afro curled up beside them, snoring lightly. Two days later, exiting her dorm room, Naomi nearly tripped over a small blue Igloo cooler. Inside, surrounded by dry ice and hooked up to a six-volt battery, she discovered the still-beating heart of a rhesus monkey.

"Here we are," Naomi says, unclasping the locket suspended from her neck, opening it, handing it to Mickey. "That's us back then."

Mickey glances from the road ahead to the small oval pictures framed in gold and back again. Young Frank is dark and classically handsome. Young Naomi is a budding flower. Their faces are eager, their potential undeniable.

"Nice," Mickey says, pulling into the driveway. "Thank you."

Night has dropped its velvet curtain over Tampa, and Mickey finds that the Steins' living room feels less like a terrarium in the dark. He and Naomi don't bother turning on the light. They sit side by side on a piece of sectional, examining the tall windows, which stare back at them blankly. Percocet notwithstanding, Mickey has another erection.

"What now, Mr. Mercer?" says Naomi.

"Mickey."

"Mickey."

He turns to her. "Where does Frank keep his files?"

"His files?"

"His documents. Journals, records, notes. That type of thing."

Naomi places a hand on Mickey's knee. "Down in the basement."

"I think it's time," Mickey says, "that we had a look at your husband's lab."

"No."

"But isn't that where he constructed the creature?"

Naomi nods. Her hand starts sliding up Mickey's thigh.

"And don't you imagine," he says, "that the lab might contain clues to his whereabouts?"

Naomi's hand stops. "Clues to whose whereabouts?"

Mickey hesitates. "The monster's whereabouts."

Naomi's hand starts moving again. "I don't like going down there," she says.

"Why not?"

"Frank says it's dangerous."

"How so?"

"It's full of hazardous chemicals and ancient, complicated equipment. If I started fooling around with something and got hurt, Frank would never forgive himself."

"But you're a smart woman," Mickey says. "Too smart to let that happen."

"There's another reason," Naomi says.

"Oh?"

She presses close to Mickey. Her hand hovers over his crotch. Her lips graze his earlobe. "It's the monster," she says. "The monster loves me. If I gave it the chance, Frank's creature would ravish me."

Divested of clothing, Naomi Stein is proportional perfection. Her skin and hair and teeth glow in the dark. She straddles Mickey on the sectional and arches her back, her rhythms orchestrated by nature, dictated by the tides. Mickey doesn't think he's ever felt anything as heavenly as the tight swaddle of her cunt. He marvels at how goddamned hard he is, considering the Percocet. Even after they've both come—Naomi with a strange, inhuman cry followed by a whimper—even as they lie curled together afterward, Mickey refrains from asking Naomi if she imagines that, in raping her, her husband's creature would recognize her as a discrete individual or would merely be satisfying a base impulse.

"What's this?" Naomi says, touching the deep divot in Mickey's right side.

"A scar."

"What happened?"

"I got shot."

"When?"

"Three months ago. Doctors couldn't remove the bullet. It's sitting against my spine."

"Goodness," Naomi says, lightly caressing the divot. "Who shot you?"

Mickey sees the split-level ranch house from a distance, as though on a drive-in screen. He sees himself in the glow of a streetlamp, entering the dwelling he shared with Rita for twenty-six years. He sees Rita standing in shadow at the bottom of the staircase, wearing a white nightgown, lifting her right arm, squeezing the trigger. He sees himself going down, sees his wife rushing to his side, kneeling. *Oh, Mickey,* she says. *I'm so sorry. I didn't know it was you. Honest. I didn't know. I thought . . . oh God, Mickey, I thought you were some kind of monster.* He sees himself losing consciousness; he sees Rita placing the gun on the foyer table; he sees his wife exiting the house, never to return.

"An intruder," Mickey says to Naomi. "I was shot by an intruder."

"You poor man," says Naomi, and Mickey feels her body tense. She pushes up to a seated position, rises to her lovely feet. She pads over dense sea-foam carpeting, stands naked before one of the windows, peering out. "Do you hear something?"

Mickey's about to say no, but then he does hear something. A sound other than the tide that keeps rushing through his head. A rustling, a stirring, a swish. The murmur of multiple feet moving through tall grass. As Mickey stands, as he moves toward Naomi, a bright spot appears in the distance. This beacon is joined by another, and another. Outside flares spark to life with increasing rapidity. These glimmers remind Mickey of a candlelit procession and seem to be swelling in size, moving closer. Mickey counts a half dozen, a dozen, two dozen.

"What's going on?" he says.

Naomi doesn't answer. She's wrapped both arms around her torso. Mickey reaches for one of her hands, peels it away from her body. It sits in his palm like a hunk of meat. Like something dead. Mickey doesn't remember her skin being so cold.

"Naomi," he says, "what the hell is this?"

"They're coming," she says.

"Who?"

"The Tampans."

"Residents of Tampa?"

Naomi nods.

"What do they want?"

"I'm guessing," she says, "that they've come for Frank's monster."

The Tampans carry torches and various household implements—pitchforks, hammers, rakes, axes, hoes. As they crowd around the floor-to-ceiling windows, Mickey sees that their suntanned faces are twisted into masks of rage. They're shouting, but their voices are muffled by the glass. The dull sound washes over Mickey like an angry tide. The Tampans start pounding with fists, then with weapons. In the glow of their torches, Mickey manages to read their lips. He makes out the words *monster* and *die,* the words *blood* and *fiend.*

"But there is no monster," he says.

Naomi backs away from the windows. Mickey's still holding her hand, and he spins her toward him. The mob gathered outside continues assaulting the glass with pitchfork handles and axes.

"Naomi," Mickey says, "talk to these people. Tell them there's nothing inhuman in this house."

"Mickey," she says, "I can't do that."

She lifts her chin, and Mickey studies her face carefully. In the sinister flicker of torchlight, he thinks he sees something strange: a seam running along her jawline.

"I don't understand," he says.

"I think you do."

A pane shatters, then another. Shards rain into the living room, splinters that sparkle in the torchlight. The roar grows deafening. The Tampans are shouting, muscling their way inside. They grab seashells, figurines, family photos. They hurl these delicate items against the walls. As three large men stomp through the glass-topped coffee table, Naomi tugs Mickey from the room. They race through the darkened house. In the kitchen, Naomi presses something hard and spiny into Mickey's hands. She flings open the back door, shoves him. "Go," she says. "Get out of here."

"What about you?"

She shakes her head.

"Frank's gone," Mickey says. "He's not coming back."

"I know."

"So come with me."

"I can't."

"Why in hell not?"

"Because," Naomi says, "I'm responsible."

"For what?"

"People make each other, Mickey. *Couples* make each other. And Frank and I are no exception."

"What are you talking about?"

She's standing two steps above Mickey, and she bends, slowly, at the waist. Seizes Mickey's biceps. Presses one of her cheeks to his. A pleasant tingle floods Mickey—the flutter of Naomi's long lashes beating against his skin, not unlike the wings of an insect. Trapped, dying, imprisoned behind a wall of glass.

"Oh, Mickey," she says, "don't you see? We're all gods. And all monsters."

From a stand of cypresses a half-mile distant, Mickey watches flames feed on the stucco walls and terra-cotta roof tiles. The .38 slug bites into his spine, but Mickey's stash of Percocet is in the pocket of his trousers, trousers he last saw balled up on the Steins' living room carpet. Mickey stands in the cypress grove, naked, shivering. He's debating running back, braving the conflagration for his painkillers and his clothes, when he looks down and sees the queen conch shell Naomi handed him as she hustled him out. Mickey lifts the shell to his ear. He hears the rush of the sea, and the inferno before him vanishes. A beach takes its place.

The sun is sinking; the tide is rolling in; Rita is there, in a white nightgown, racing along the shoreline. A colossal creature is chasing her—an inhuman monster assembled from spare parts inexpertly sewn together. Mickey starts to call out a warning, but he realizes the creature isn't menacing his wife. She and the monster are laughing. Moving in tandem across wet sand. Frolicking in the swells. Making Mickey feel like an intruder. He wants to tell Rita she was right. To tell her he forgives her. To beg her to come back. But he's afraid of her response, so he watches her cavort with another monster in the pounding surf, which wipes away their footprints as soon as they appear.

The Tepid Tears of Orphans

Yet Dives himself, he too lives like a Czar in an ice palace made of frozen sighs, and being a president of a temperance society, he only drinks the tepid tears of orphans.

—Herman Melville, *Moby-Dick*

You've got me mixed up with someone else, Roland says from the bird-shit-painted stoop on which he holds court whenever he's not eating or sleeping or pimp-limping down the block, arm swinging, oily hair center-parted, teeth blinging, downy hairs peppering his upper lip, murmuring to spectral drifters about the quality of his product, sighing to honey-skinned mamas about the size of his dick. *I only take cash.* But when you pull the vial from the pocket of the threadbare trench you stripped off Anita—who, God rest her, no longer needs it—and hold it aloft so that its clear contents glint in the milky, semiprecious winter light, Roland is visibly intrigued. Briny air blasts in from the waterfront five blocks distant as he rises from the stoop, hitching up the jeans in which his spindly boy legs swim. His posse rises with him—Ray-Ray, Big Steve, and Jesse, who once said you remind him of a junkie that lived in his building when he was growing up, a woman who gave him clandestine laundry room blowjobs. Once, as he dropped his pants in an alley off Third, as your head bobbed between his legs, Jesse said that, for him, fellatio will forever conjure up the scent of Bounce. But he doesn't look at you now; Jesse's blank eyes roam over tagged stoops and crowded row houses as Roland plucks the vial from your fingers, holds it close to his pockmarked face. *How the fuck you get so many?* he says, but you just shrug, unwilling to give up your secrets, unable to speak lest you crumble, something you must never do in front of them. Roland demands temperance of everyone in his crew; as a result, his ship is the tightest-run in the city. He can't be tempted by conventional highs, this man-child, but in his face—in the set line of his jaw—you see that he wants what you're pushing. *Give her three bags for it,* he grunts, and as Ray-Ray rolls inside to tap the hidden stash, anticipatory saliva floods your mouth. Your bowels hum, zing, clench. Your tainted flesh cries out for relief, but before you scurry back to the dingy room in which you've left not only your works but also Anita's children—Travis and Tina—sobbing over their mother's stiffening remains, you watch Roland uncap the vial. His entourage hangs, suspended in a loose cluster, as he lifts the glass bottle to his lips. Once it's empty, you see how the ingestion of such elemental anguish has changed him, and you know Roland is hooked. From now on, he'll be crippled. Consumed by a thirst that can never be quenched. As you fly through the streets, rushing toward the residential hotel in which, ten years ago, you met Anita—the flophouse that has become her tomb—you wonder how long your supply can possibly hold out. How many tears Travis and Tina will shed for their departed mother. What steps you might take to prolong their sorrow.

Iphigenia in Baltimore

Sing to me, O Muse, of Beatrice Fleck, thirty-six-year-old virginal fourth-grade teacher, strongest woman alive, and covert author of erotic novelettes. Unsullied not by choice but by the inscrutable designs of fate, Beatrice wanted nothing more than to be plundered. Despoiled. Sacked. Even as she stood before a roomful of nine-year-olds, elucidating the rudiments of multidigit multiplication, even as she monitored the playground monkey bars, Beatrice dreamed of a skirted, sandaled hero climbing her ramparts. Looting her hallowed heights. A man over whom some god had cast a glamour, one that made him sturdy enough to contend with Beatrice, whose paranormal strength had come to light when she was but a spindly six-year-old, the day an upright piano collapsed on her teacher, Mr. Phelps, pinning him to the tiled floor of his bachelor apartment.

Beatrice, who loved Mr. Phelps, pushed aside the instrument as though it were made of balsa wood. She scooped up her teacher, tossed him over her shoulder in a fireman's carry, and scurried toward the office of the town's physician, Dr. Mort Beckman. Those who hadn't seen the forty-pound child carrying a grown man like a sack of flour had soon heard about it, and from that day forward, Beatrice was a local curio. Thirty years later, she'd put a thousand miles between herself and her Midwestern origin. She lived in Baltimore, where no one knew of her freakish strength. No one knew that she spent her solitary nights constructing naughty narratives, that even while delivering lectures on the customs and daily lives of Native Americans she was thinking of erect nipples and engorged members listing to starboard, straining at the zippers of tight dungarees.

"Ms. Fleck, what's a dungaree?"

Beatrice's class tittered.

"I wasn't talking about *dungarees.* I was definitely talking about *tepees.* Manny Alvarez, please tell the class what I said about tepees."

But Manny, secretly Beatrice's favorite student, couldn't answer, because Ms. Fleck hadn't mentioned tepees for nearly two minutes. She'd been talking instead about a young widow and the man who cleaned her pool, a man who wrote poetry and wore tight dungarees. As Ms. Fleck had paced the front of the classroom, painting a vivid picture of the pair, the class stopped squirming and doodling and whispering. They sat at rapt attention, small hands folded in front of them, gazing at skinny, fluttery Ms. Fleck. Her kinky hair was the color of rust, her lips a dark shade of pink. She never got angry like the other teachers, never raised her voice, and she was exceptionally good at explaining things. All the students were fond of her, but Manny loved her. Her green eyes pleaded silently for his help, and he cast around for something to say about tepees.

"Um, tepees were cone-shaped?" Manny said. "And covered in buffalo hide?"

Ms. Fleck's gaze was full of appreciation, and she nodded. Just then the classroom door opened. Nathaniel Baxter stuck his head inside. "Ms. Fleck," he said, "may I have a word?"

Nathaniel Baxter taught English at the high school next door. Twenty-five years older than Beatrice, he was tall, with lustrous silver hair and large, lovely teeth. Lately, whenever Beatrice sat down at her laptop to write about illicit motel meetings and kisses stolen on cross-country trains, the man she started out envisioning dissolved into Nathaniel. "This man," her editor said, when he called to discuss her latest manuscript, "don't you think he's a bit old to be an Olympic diver?" And he was, but Beatrice couldn't get Nathaniel out of her mind.

He'd come from Connecticut, where he'd lived for thirty years, teaching literature and raising a family. When an affair with a doctoral candidate writing her dissertation on Euripides went awry, derailing marriage and career, Nathaniel retreated to the city of his birth, where he took a job teaching public school. On a crisp October evening, he read his poetry at a downtown coffeehouse. Beatrice sat at the back, where the dulcet tones of Nathaniel's voice touched her physically. Each time his gray eyes rose from the lectern to skim the crowd, she trembled. His poems concerned epic quests and intertextuality and algorithms and language in transition, and they all seemed to Beatrice tinged with sorrow, and she thought about cradling his silver head in her lap. She thought about wearing a pinafore and carrying a picnic basket. She thought about making love in a field of sunflowers. After the reading, Nathaniel asked her out for a drink, and Beatrice sat riveted, nursing a light beer and listening to him hold forth on poetry and marriage and loneliness. She was tempted to tell him that she, too, was a writer, but she worried that Nathaniel Baxter might scoff at her bawdy scribblings. He escorted her home, where he leaned in for a kiss. Her heart thudded as he asked if she was going to invite him inside. She wanted to—she'd cleaned her apartment that day on the off chance that this fantasy might actually come true—but Beatrice was afraid. It was fear that had preserved her maidenhood—not of sex but of doing bodily harm, a fear hanging over her ever since she paralyzed a boy named Roy Tanner.

As a girl, Beatrice defeated all comers at arm wrestling and lifted whatever people asked her to—washing machines, refrigerators, pickup trucks. The high school coach tried to recruit her for football and wrestling, but Beatrice didn't want to do battle; she wanted to be loved. Adored like Mimi Falcon and Jess Carter, whose delicate feet never touched the ground, who were held always aloft on a buoyant cloud of admiration. The boys in her hometown were afraid of Beatrice, so it wasn't until she fled to college in Maryland, where no one guessed at the aberrant strength concealed within her willowy frame, that she was even kissed.

Throughout freshman year she dated a boy named Roy Tanner, and by the time they were naked on the twin bed in his dorm room, a sock hung on the doorknob despite the fact that his roommate was home for the weekend, Beatrice feared she might erupt. She often wondered if the ache that throbbed through her at the sight of the male anatomy was part of her condition, if the hardening of her nipples and the drenching of her panties were further proof of her freakishness. Roy whipped her into a froth with fingers, lips, and tongue, but also with words, dirty things whispered unceasingly into her ear. "You're so wet, baby," he would say, "like Niagara Falls." Or, guiding her hand to his swollen penis, he would whisper, "Can't you feel how bad I want to be inside you?" But what Beatrice liked most was his talk of popping her cherry. The idea of a ripe, red cherry hidden inside her, one Roy could obliterate with a single stroke, drove her mad, and by the time he slid down her panties, by the time he positioned his angular hips between her thighs, she lost all control. Wrapping her legs around him, she clasped him to her with every ounce of her inhuman strength. She heard a wicked crack and a series of crunches, and Roy shrieked, and Beatrice spent the rest of the night in the ER waiting room. When they let her in to see Roy—his pelvis and lower vertebrae were crushed and six ribs broken—he averted his eyes. Gazing through the window at the rose-red rising sun, he said he wanted nothing more to do with her.

"I can't," Beatrice had said to Nathaniel at her front door, the night of the poetry reading, hoping he would assume she had her period or hadn't shaved her legs and not that she didn't want him. She longed for him in the way that, as a girl, she'd longed for the power of flight. Once he left, she worked on her latest novelette, the tale of a chorus girl and a veteran Broadway producer. In bed, she climaxed to thoughts of Nathaniel, recalling the ambrosial taste of his lips and the way his voice rippled through the coffee shop. Beatrice didn't use a vibrator to bring herself to orgasm, only the expert fingers of her right hand. Over the years she'd considered purchasing an implement, had perused them in shops, but until she could safely usher an actual penis inside her, Beatrice was determined to keep her cherry intact.

"I'll be back in a moment, class," Ms. Fleck said before ducking into the hall with Mr. Baxter. "Work on your long division. Manny, please write on the blackboard the name of any student who talks."

But Manny Alvarez wasn't paying attention to who was talking in Ms. Fleck's classroom. Everyone was, it seemed, or maybe no one. Manny didn't care. He didn't like Mr. Baxter and wished he could wipe him from the face of the earth. Manny's father would have called Mr. Baxter a dog. He would have said Mr. Baxter came sniffing around Ms. Fleck like she was a bitch in heat. When you loved a woman, like Manny's father had loved his mother, you didn't let dogs sniff around her. You kicked them until they took off with their tails between their legs.

"Ms. Fleck and Mr. Baxter, sitting in a tree, K-I-S-S-I-N-G."

"You think she likes him?"

"No way. He's like her grandpa."

"How old is Ms. Fleck?"

"I don't know. Twenty?"

When Ms. Fleck returned, her cheeks were flushed and she was smiling too widely. There were no names on the blackboard. "I thought I heard voices," Ms. Fleck said, walking around the classroom. She stopped behind Manny and touched his shoulder. She knelt beside his desk. "Manny, did I hear voices?"

"No, Ms. Fleck," he said, but he knew that she knew he was lying. Beatrice and Manny could communicate without words. Beatrice thought it was because Manny was so mature, but Manny knew it was because Ms. Fleck was so innocent.

"All right, class," she said, straightening up, "who can tell me how many times eleven goes into three hundred and ninety-six?"

As she watched five students attempt to work the problem on the board, Beatrice tried to slow the flutter of her heart. She knew Nathaniel's reputation. She'd heard the chatter in the teachers' lounge. She knew he'd taken out Virginia Gordon, who taught fifth grade, and Katie Knight, the Spanish teacher at the high school. Melanie Thomas, who worked in the front office, and Janine Matson, the vice principal. Rumor had it that the dalliance with the doctoral candidate had been far from his first. Coeds. Adjunct professors. School administrators. Dozens, maybe hundreds. Beatrice was aware of these things. They were, in part, what drew her to Nathaniel. What made her decide, as she stood in front of her nine-year-olds, as they kicked their restless feet and stuck out their tongues and wiggled in their seats, that he was the one.

In the hall, he'd asked her to dinner that night. She would invite him back to her apartment. She would pour a decent red. She would put on a Marvin Gaye album and turn down the lights. She would straddle him on the sofa. She would not allow herself to become overexcited. She would remind herself to go slow, to be gentle. Over the years, Beatrice had tried many times to will away her brute strength. To divorce herself from it. Shed it like a lizard's skin. She found this to be impossible, however. Not that it was all bad. At times she rather liked being so powerful. She never had trouble opening a jar of peanut butter, and carrying groceries to her fourth-floor walk-up was no sweat. And when the gray Baltimore winter finally melted into spring, she ran for miles at top speed without tiring. But these things couldn't outweigh what her strength had done to her love life.

Since Roy Tanner, she'd come close to intercourse on several occasions, but as the moment of penetration drew near, Beatrice always felt herself slipping, losing the control she was generally able to exert. Roy's shattered body floated inevitably into her mind, and she was forced to halt the proceedings. After one particularly frustrating near miss, she sat down and banged out her first novelette, the story of a buttoned-up schoolteacher and an oily auto mechanic. Afterward, it was as though an erotic muse had claimed Beatrice as her mouthpiece—a muse who flooded her with an in-depth understanding of what it was like to be normal.

But it had been years since she'd gotten close to a man, and Beatrice felt it was now or never. The only way to go into this was with eyes wide open, so she would tell Nathaniel about her unnatural strength. What she did to Roy Tanner. Her writings. Her virginity. It would be a relief to reveal these things, to share the burden of her peculiar truths. It was only fair to give Nathaniel the facts and let *him* weigh the risks. And though Beatrice's experience with men was mostly fictitious, though she dealt almost exclusively in fantasies, she was sure that Nathaniel Baxter would fall in line. That he would risk his well-being to have a go at her. It was this conviction, as much as his silver hair and sweet voice, that drew Beatrice so strongly.

At dinner, when he asked about her writings, Beatrice would say her stories were born of her desire to struggle weakly against a man, to swipe at him like a feeble kitten, to forget that she could, at any moment, choose to overpower him.

"Ms. Fleck?"

Manny stood before her. At the bell, she'd dismissed the class and sunk into her chair. The boy's bright, dark eyes bored into her.

"Yes? What is it?"

He stepped forward, pressing his thin body into her desk. He reached both arms across its scarred surface. Beatrice's hands, which showed her age more than any other part of her, rested palms up on the blotter. Manny grasped them and squeezed. Beatrice was momentarily undone.

"Thank you, Manny," she said.

Manny had first followed Ms. Fleck home months earlier, and on many an evening, after he finished his homework and fixed himself hot dogs or a can of ravioli for supper, he would make his way to her building. He only had to take one bus to get there. Ms. Fleck lived on the fourth floor of a not-so-nice place by the standards of most white people, but it was nicer than the building he and his mother had moved into a year earlier, six months after his father, a longshoreman, was crushed by a shipping container filled with stereo equipment. From across the street, Manny could see into Ms. Fleck's window. She never pulled the shades, and every time Manny had been there, she was sitting at a card table pushed close to the glass, typing on a laptop. There was a mailbox on the corner, and Manny liked to clamber onto it and sit, rhythmically kicking the blue metal, watching, and think about the two of them living in one of the tepees she was forever talking about. They would wear loincloths, which would leave Ms. Fleck's breasts swinging free. Manny would stalk elk, deer, bison. Once he speared them, once he skinned and hacked them into manageable hunks of meat, Ms. Fleck would roast the flesh over a blazing fire. They would gather fruits and nuts and berries. They would tan the hides and then stretch them over frames to make drums. They would dry empty gourds and fill them with seeds. They would pound the drums and shake the gourds while dancing around the fire, praying for rain and whatever else they needed. Ms. Fleck would never be too tired to listen. She would place his hands on her breasts, leading him gently into manhood. Manny's mother didn't get home from second shift at the blanket factory until two a.m., and Manny would sometimes sit on the mailbox watching Ms. Fleck until after midnight, wondering what would happen if she turned out her desk lamp and caught sight of him down below.

After she showered and wriggled into a low-cut aquamarine dress, Beatrice stood at her window. It was still light out, and someone was moving into the top floor of the building across the street. Walking home from school, she'd seen movers using a block and tackle to hoist an upright piano. The instrument now hung midair. It would never fit, Beatrice could see that, and she wondered what kind of movers would hoist a piano without first measuring the window. Night was falling, and the brawny men were nowhere to be seen. Was it to be left suspended overnight? This worried Beatrice, but when she caught sight of Nathaniel Baxter approaching her building, she forgot about the instrument.

In the restaurant, an Italian place to which Nathaniel always took his dates, he ordered a bottle of decent red and wondered what he'd done to deserve Beatrice Fleck. He'd last deflowered a girl twenty years earlier, a sophomore named Mandy who cried afterward. Nathaniel cried, too—he was nothing if not empathetic—and held Mandy until she drifted to sleep. He even remained stretched beside her on the dorm room twin for a time, listening to the whistle of her breath, watching her small breasts rise and fall. If he'd known she would be his last virgin, Nathaniel might have spent the whole night with Mandy, but he had an eight a.m. class that semester—a seminar on Homer, Virgil, and Dante. As he scuttled through his forties and fifties, Nathaniel never managed to talk his way into the pants of another unsullied girl, and as he'd now entered his sixties, that fantasy was long behind him. But here, out of the clear blue, was his very own *Beatrice,* a virgin offering herself up like Iphigenia, the innocent whose spilled blood Artemis demanded before she would allow Agamemnon and the Achaean fleet to sail in pursuit of Menelaus's wayward wife. True, Beatrice was older than your average virgin, but she looked ten years younger than her age, Nathaniel thought, and when she declared that she wanted him to take her maidenhood that very night, Sir Penis, that one-eyed showstopper, who these days did not always obey commands, stood at full attention, knocking against the bottom of the table, throbbing with such force that Nathaniel was tempted to sweep away the glasses and bread plates and butter pats and take Beatrice Fleck right there. Even when she announced that she was cursed with abnormal strength, that she remained a virgin because she'd paralyzed the only man she ever came close to screwing, Nathaniel wasn't deterred. He was used to girls with crazy notions; unstable women are the cornerstone of the adulterous relationship. The more he gazed at Beatrice, the lovelier she grew. He wanted to sit at her feet and bury his head in her lap. He silently thanked the gods for this unexpected boon, promising them burnt offerings, the fatty thighs of rams and hogs or whatever else they desired.

"There's something else," Beatrice said. She leaned across the table. "I write erotica."

Nathaniel nearly swooned. He downed his water in three gulps and the waiter hurried to refill his glass. Beatrice pulled a thin paperback from her handbag and slid it across the table. Nathaniel greedily skimmed the first paragraph his eyes found:

> The rocker was one of a set Philip and his wife purchased on holiday in Martha's Vineyard thirty years earlier: sturdy boughs of walnut, an intricately caned seat. In it, on countless evenings, Philip had rocked two infant sons into sweet slumber, and he felt that he knew this chair better than any other. When he shared it with Ivy, when she hiked up her plaid skirt and straddled him, rocking them softly with the tips of her exquisite toes, brushing her glossed lips against his, separated from him by one thin layer of cotton and one of gabardine, Philip prayed for death. He prayed for a masked intruder to creep up behind him, to sink a knife between his shoulder blades. He wanted to be forever suspended here, at the apex of experience, where things take shape and become possible. For Philip, the anticipation was far more rapturous than the act.

"Jesus," Nathaniel said. He'd expected Beatrice's narrative to be titillating; he hadn't expected it to reach through his V-neck sweater and thump his heart. On the book's cover, an illustrated man embraced an illustrated woman from behind. He was shirtless and she wore a man's white button-down. Superimposed over this was a drawing of an empty rocking chair. Nathaniel looked up at Beatrice, who was ordering chicken marsala from the waiter, and understood that he was dealing with a profounder mystery than he'd imagined.

Though the restaurant was some distance from Beatrice's building, the March night was warm, and they chose to walk. As Nathaniel listened to Beatrice talk of the town where she grew up and the characters who populated her fourth-grade class, he rolled up his sleeves. The wind was high, and he was preternaturally aware of the night air. His eyes roamed over brick and stone facades, over bodegas and newsstands, and he wondered why he'd always thought Baltimore so grim. The city seemed, in this moment, softened and brightened. Drenched with possibility. Streetlamps and traffic lights twinkled. The people they passed were all attractive. Laughter rang out. Music with no visible source followed them over the sidewalk, a melody sweet and filled with yearning. Nathaniel felt as though it might take days to reach their destination, and he found that he didn't mind.

Eventually they arrived at Beatrice's building, whose bohemian charm reminded Nathaniel of the tatty dwellings of other girls he'd loved. Feeling like a teenager, he chased Beatrice up four flights, wondering at his own stamina. In her apartment, she pushed him down on the sofa and sat astride him. They proceeded toward their common goal with painstaking care. Beatrice shed her clothes, and he was mystified. Dressed, she seemed fragile, easily broken, but now he saw that her shoulders were broad, that her body rippled with muscles. Her breasts stood up like two ripe apples, and her jutting hip bones were the prettiest things he'd ever seen. In spite of her probing tongue, her roving fingers, Nathaniel sensed reluctance in Beatrice Fleck, and to his surprise, he felt a hesitancy of his own.

"We can stay here," he whispered as his hand slid incrementally up her thigh. "We don't have to go any further. We can stay right here forever."

Beatrice, who sat on his lap, gave a quizzical look. "Don't be silly," she said. "I'll be right back."

Once she left the room, Nathaniel stood. His erection throbbed, and he crossed to the open window. He thought he'd never wanted any woman as much as he wanted Beatrice. He peered through the screen, amazed by the strength of his vision, which was sharper than it had been in fifteen years. He took note of the things that made this night unique, things he would cherish when he looked back as the self he would become in the future, when he wanted to relive his time with Beatrice Fleck. A fat woman walking an unclipped standard poodle. A convertible full of shrieking teenagers. A man balancing on his hands. A small boy sitting atop mailbox, glaring up at Nathaniel. An upright piano tied with stout ropes, dangling in midair above the mailbox, swaying in the wind.

"My gods," he said to Beatrice, who entered the room exactly as a sickening crack sounded, as the massive wooden block holding the piano in place splintered.

Later, Manny Alvarez would hardly remember the crack. He would hardly remember the piano. He would hardly remember Mr. Baxter's hateful face staring back at him from Ms. Fleck's window. He would hardly remember Ms. Fleck materializing beside him, lifting her arms, bending her knees, catching the piano over her head, grunting softly, fighting for balance, holding the instrument aloft for a moment before kneeling to place it on the sidewalk. What Manny *would* remember was the way Ms. Fleck's breasts bounced as she caught and then discarded the piano, how they pressed against him when she snatched him from the mailbox and held him so that he couldn't breathe.

She wore only silky purple panties, the kind his father had liked on his mother, and Ms. Fleck's pale breasts were just as Manny had imagined them. As she held him on the sidewalk, as she swayed back and forth and whispered "You're all right. Everything's all right now" into his ear, as those who'd witnessed the event ringed Beatrice and Manny, Manny felt that if he and Ms. Fleck closed their eyes and wished hard enough, they would find themselves in a clearing. Wearing loincloths and gathering wood and roasting hunks of meat and dancing around a fire.

Praying for all the things they needed.

When Beatrice walked into her apartment wearing the white button-down shirt given to her by a man who had watched her save Manny Alvarez, Nathaniel was forced to avert his eyes. Some deathless god had lavished a splendor on Beatrice. She looked taller, fuller. Encircled by a nimbus of light, she glowed. She reminded Nathaniel of Artemis, the huntress, zealously guarding her chastity with silver bow and arrow, and he trembled.

"What is it?" Beatrice said. "What's wrong?"

"Nothing," he said. "I should go."

"Please don't."

"I should," Nathaniel said, but he didn't move.

"Is this about my strength?" Beatrice said. "You didn't believe me before. And now you're frightened."

Nathaniel was frightened, yes, but not in the way she thought. He wasn't frightened of what *she* could do to *him* but of what *he* could do to *her*. Of how the man who destroyed her maidenhead would change the world. As he'd watched Beatrice manhandle the piano and avert disaster, understanding struck Nathaniel like one of Zeus's bolts. Her strength was tied to her purity. Had he deflowered her before the instrument plummeted, she would have been unable to save the child. Beatrice Fleck should never be forfeited for the sake of one man's vanity and pride.

"In some versions of the story," he said, "Iphigenia is not sacrificed. Artemis snatches her from the altar and leaves a deer in her place."

On the sofa, Beatrice cradled Nathaniel's silver head in her lap. She expected to feel frustrated, thwarted. Instead, it was as though she'd been given a reprieve. She smiled at Nathaniel, whose eyes were changed, lit with awe. A new story occurred to her, one whose eroticism lay beneath the surface. A story in which men journey from far and wide to fall at the feet of a woman who, they believe, can destroy the world as they know it with one finger snap, one eyeblink. They're willing to sacrifice themselves, these men, willing to march single file off a cliff or have their hearts torn out and eaten by the priests of her order. For they believe in her strength, in the great, undeniable force of her. They believe if they pray hard enough, if they feed her enough of their lives, she will grant them all they desire.

When Dawn reached her rosy fingers into Beatrice Fleck's apartment, she found Beatrice seated at her laptop, typing in a rhythmic fury. Nathaniel Baxter lay on the sofa, dreaming of his gods. All day, the sun dangled like a ripe, red cherry in the sky.

Well-Built Men, 18 to 30, Who Would Like to Be Eaten by Me

You find it in Tristan's room, an ad excised from the personals, folded in even thirds, tucked into a collection of South American folktales. The book was a gift from Tristan's first boss, the *capitán* of a Bolivian crew that once cleaned his father's law office. Tristan was nineteen then, the youngest of four boys, a rising college sophomore home for summer break, and you thought the janitorial job beneath him. But when you pointed this out to Dean, who'd not yet left you for his twenty-year-old paralegal, who'd not yet discovered that within his colon a malignant mass was marshaling its fatal forces, your then-husband seized your slight shoulders. *You've got to face facts, Connie,* he said. *The boy's never been right.* It was true that Tristan was always unnaturally attached, that unlike his brothers, who blazed trails toward wives, children, careers in periodontal care and hunger relief, Tristan always clung to you, hid in your shadows. He was the only one to show interest in your former life as a human oddity, a contortionist known on the southeastern carnival circuit as Collapsible Connie. Your specialty was dislocating your shoulders, folding your limbs, knitting your bones into an impossible rectangle of humanity, one small enough to stuff inside a lockbox. You learned the secrets of escaping such a prison from your uncle Mesmer, a tiny man who sprang from the heart of the Bolivian rain forest, spawned by the chieftain of a purportedly anthropophagous tribe. When you were twelve, Mesmer was devoured by a docile lion named Daphne, and for years afterward, when no one was looking, you would sneak off to Daphne's cage, pry open her colossal jaws, lay your head against the rough pillow of her tongue. *Go on,* you would whisper, *take me, too.* But you received in response only a humming purr. Tristan was the only person to whom you revealed this, the only person to whom you admitted that, at zoos, you never stopped jealously eyeing the raw meat fed to big cats. From the moment you first held your youngest, you understood that he'd inherited your flexibility, and you taught him everything you know about contortion, about compliance. Seven years after Tristan received his BA in anthropology, Dean was consumed by cancer, and since your ex-husband never got around to marrying his poor paralegal, his money went to your sons. You and Tristan pooled your resources and, on the twenty-eighth anniversary of his birth, put down a deposit on this Craftsman bungalow. Three days ago, your son departed for an overnight camping trip, and he hasn't returned. When you invade the sanctity of his room, you discover the personal ad, and your eyes feast on the unnatural words. You think of Shirley Loomis, who once informed you that, while spending the night at her house, your ten-year-old son begged her boy Jimmy to eat him. *Please,* Tristan said. *Swallow my flesh.* You never mentioned this to Dean; even you and Tristan never discussed your shared desire to be ingested, to escape this mortal cage via esophagus, stomach, intestines. And now, rather than calling the police, you find yourself collapsing, folding your limbs, knitting up your bones. You cower on the carpet, the slightest version of yourself, wondering when Tristan emerged from your shadows. At what point you crawled into his.

Rebirth of the Big Top

Miranda the Elephant Girl was the first of them. Trevor hired her to work concessions on Fridays and alternate Wednesdays. "I cannot cook, and I don't do windows," she'd joked in halting English. "Anything else, I'm your girl." Trevor guessed she was pushing forty. She wore cutoff dungarees and a half-shirt, making no attempt to hide her condition. From a distance, the skin of her arms, legs, and torso looked filthy, or like the spotted pelt of a jaguar. Close up, rough gray scales leaped into focus. Trevor perched on the edge of his battered desk, watching her stare down the box fan that circulated stifling air through his office, words like *armored* and *stegosaurus* and *parched* scuttling through his brain. The skin of her back resembled a relief map of a locale he'd never imagined.

Gill Nathan's World-Famous Carnival and Sideshow had been touring the Southeast when an aneurysm erupted in Gill Nathan's brain, killing him, stranding his employees outside Atlanta. Trapeze artists and lion tamers. Strongmen and acrobats. Bareback riders and clowns. A whole slew of human oddities.

"I cannot tell you how much appreciation I feel," Miranda said, as Trevor showed her how to load and operate the popcorn popper, how to change the soda syrup and deal with the sticky drawer on the cash register. "Most of us have never known any other life. It would be nice if you could hire more of my colleagues."

But no one came to the drive-in. Trevor couldn't even afford the Elephant Girl. He wasn't sure why he'd hired her in the first place.

Cassie hadn't had the strength to see it through. Trevor had read as much in a note she'd affixed to the white door of the Frigidaire on a Monday morning in April. Joshua had just turned twelve. When Trevor touched the sleeping boy's shoulder, Josh's sunken blue eyes snapped open.

"She's gone?"

Trevor nodded.

Josh struggled to a seated position. "Where do you think she'll go?"

"California? It's where all the beautiful people end up."

That morning, Trevor quit his job in order to take over the boy's schooling. "Are you crazy?" Nick Peterson said. "You're the best we've got. You were born to do this."

Trevor had always had a knack for turning failing businesses around. When he was eight, the addition of fresh lime to his lemonade made his the busiest stand in a twelve-block radius. At ten, he'd suggested that his uncle knock a hole in the south wall of his casual dining restaurant to install a drive-through, and sales at Carl's Cozy Corner had tripled. And for his father, a furrier who hawked the pelts of rabbits, minks, and foxes in the viscous atmosphere of north Georgia, Trevor's myriad suggestions—layaway, soft lighting, comfy chairs, cool drinks—added up to pure profit. As a consultant with the Atlanta firm of Dowd, Dowd, and Blessing, Trevor had traveled the country for ten years, studying business plans and cost analyses, telling people from all walks of life how to run their enterprises better. On average, he increased profitability by an astounding

57 percent—twice the percentage achieved by any other D, D, and B consultant.

"We could go under without you," Nick Peterson pleaded.

"Sorry," Trevor said. "My priority is the boy."

Cassie had been gone a month when Josh announced that he might like to see California. Trevor had just finished stirring Vermont maple syrup into Josh's oatmeal. When he lifted a napkin to wipe a glob from the boy's chin, an unexpected sob tore from Trevor, like pressurized molten matter escaping a volcano.

"Shh," Josh said, placing a withered hand on his father's arm. "We're OK."

In terms of hair, Josh had only ever had a thin fringe hugging the outside of his enormous cranium. His body was the brittlest thing Trevor had ever touched. The wrinkling of his skin had started a couple years earlier. Sometime in the next year, he would most likely suffer a fatal heart attack.

That afternoon they studied geography. Trevor spread a map of the United States across the kitchen table, and he and Josh pushed Matchbox cars from state to state, memorizing capitals. Each state was a particular shade of blue; these tonal variations roiled over the map like ocean waves. Josh had spent his entire life in Georgia. Trevor decided what he and the boy should probably do was travel.

After the Elephant Girl, Trevor hired Neil, who'd accompanied Miranda to a Wednesday shift at the concession stand. The hirsute young man closely resembled posttransformation Lon Chaney Jr. in *The Wolf Man*.

"You do not mind if he just stands beside the counter, Mr. Trevor?" Miranda had said. "Neil has nowhere to go, and he is crazy for American movies."

Trevor, too, was crazy for American movies. He figured this was why, after returning from his cross-country travels, he hadn't gone back to Dowd, Dowd, and Blessing. Why, instead, he'd taken the remainder of his savings and purchased the Big Top Drive-In, an establishment on the brink of foreclosure and collapse, twenty miles south of Atlanta. When he was a boy, his parents had often taken him to the Big Top; the cinematic outings had given his family a much-needed break, releasing the tension that forever charged the air at home. Nights at the Big Top were organized by genre: Western Wednesdays, Noir Thursdays, Romance Saturdays. Trevor knew he'd seen *Arsenic and Old Lace* on a Tuesday, *Now, Voyager* on a Saturday, *Destry Rides Again* on a Wednesday. The taste of popcorn and fountain soda, the tinny sounds that burst from the metal speaker hung on the window of his father's Buick, the sticky sensation of bare thighs against leather, the sight of his mother resting her curly head on his father's shoulder—these were the bright spots of boyhood.

When Trevor took over the Big Top, he screened the films of his youth. He reintroduced genre nights. The public stayed away in droves.

"Perhaps you should try showing something modern, Mr. Trevor?" Miranda suggested after a couple of weeks. "Shirley MacLaine and Steve McQueen. *Bye Bye Birdie.* Warren Beatty. Then the people, they might come."

Trevor set Neil up in the booth, teaching him how to run the projector, how to spot the white circle that heralds the reel change, how to load the heavy spools of film. "Where you from, Neil?" he asked.

"Upstate New York," the young man replied.

"Cold up that way."

"It's good for my condition. Better than this heat."

"What about Miranda?"

"Oh, this is the place for her. Swampy. Cold dries her out something terrible."

"You two together?"

Neil shrugged. "Sort of."

"Ever think about shaving?"

"Sure," Neil replied. "I used to. But it just keeps coming back."

Trevor had gotten his first tattoo in North Carolina. On the lower right side of his back. "Cool," Joshua had said, running his fingers over the saran-covered Tar Heel State, shaded the same blue as its counterpart on their U.S. map. "I want one."

"You're too young."

Josh looked thirty years older than his father. The absurdity of Trevor's statement wavered between them.

"Come on, Dad. What are you afraid of?"

He feared the pain that streaked his son's face as Tiny the tattoo artist injected subcutaneous ink. The burly man had hesitated for several long seconds before agreeing. "You sure he's old enough?"

Trevor looked at Josh, who peeled off his striped shirt to reveal skeletal arms, a shriveled chest and back. The boy nodded enthusiastically. Trevor turned to Tiny and did the same.

Mingled with the discomfort on Josh's face was evidence of the boy's particular and serene strength—fortitude bred from a lifelong battle with agony. As they ambled back to the Mountaineer Motor Court, something swelled inside Trevor. He swung his son high in the air, then hugged him to his chest. In cabin twelve they stood with their backs to the mirror, shirtless, peering over their shoulders, studying their matching modifications.

"Cool," Josh said again, softly.

The plan was to hit every state, driving the Chevy up the East Coast to Maine, making their way down to Alabama, then back up to Michigan, and so on. They'd set out in May. The weather was fine in Pennsylvania and New York, in Vermont and New Hampshire. They didn't spend long in each state, just time enough to see a couple sights and add a tattoo to their burgeoning body maps. Trevor estimated it would take three months to reach California.

"It's nothing like home," he told Josh. "The trees are different, and the flowers, and the animals. It's almost like another country."

"What do you think she's doing?"

Trevor couldn't imagine. When they met, Cassie had been an aesthetician with aspirations. She loved musicals—*The King and I* and *Kiss Me, Kate* and *Guys and Dolls.* She belted out numbers in the shower, while washing dishes, and behind the wheel of the car. Occasionally she would cradle Trevor's head in her lap, ruffling his thinning hair with her nervous fingers, singing softly, her eyelids low. She was too pretty for Trevor, who'd never been more than average looking. If she hadn't gotten pregnant with Joshua, Trevor doubted she would have married him. He'd been working for Dowd, Dowd, and Blessing just over a year, building his unassailable reputation, when the boy was born.

"No," Cassie had said, after Dr. Derringer sat them down. "I don't believe you."

Their son was two. By the age of seven, he would appear to be fifty. It would be a miracle if he saw thirteen.

"That's not possible," Cassie said, turning to Trevor. "Tell him Josh isn't sick. Tell him we can't watch him die. That we won't."

Dr. Derringer's office was flooded with afternoon light, but Trevor felt a fog creeping through. He thought of Max Schreck, of the eerie, jagged shade he'd cast on the walls in *Nosferatu.* The shadow of the vampire had heralded death; if it fell upon you, you were done for.

"Trevor," Cassie said, but Trevor was afraid to lift his eyes. He didn't want to look at his wife. He reached for her hand, which lay in his palm like something cold, scaly, inanimate. "Please," she'd said.

"Maybe she's working as an extra on a musical," Trevor said to Josh, as they zoomed from Kentucky into Tennessee. "Maybe she'll get picked out of the crowd when the star breaks an ankle and she'll take over the lead."

"Are you mad at her?"

"I don't know. Are you?"

Josh was eating animal crackers from one of those red circus-train-car boxes. He held up two elephants. Sitting on his knees, he walked them slowly across the dashboard of the Chevy, scooting closer and closer to Trevor. Just as the animals crested the rise over the instrument panel, Josh snatched them back and crammed them into his mouth. He pressed his heavy head into his father's upper arm.

"Yeah," he said when he finished chewing. "But I think I forgive her."

After Miranda and Neil came Julius the Lobster Man, whose hands were shaped like two crustaceous claws. Conjoined twins Sheila and Shirley shared an enlarged heart. Duane had no arms, and Ruby no legs. Gina the Giantess stood nearly seven feet tall. Bertram's parasitic twin dangled from his lower spine. Trevor gave each employee a shift a week in the concession stand or the ticket booth. Sometimes he paid them to pick up trash that nonexistent customers left. Even when they weren't working, his employees gravitated to the Big Top, where they hung around, chatting with one another, watching the movies Neil projected onto the screen: *Dr. Ehrlich's Magic Bullet. The Man Who Came to Dinner. Force of Evil.*

One night Trevor was awakened by a light scratching on his bedroom window. He rose and stumbled to the front door. His dilapidated cottage stood on the back side of the drive-in and had been included in the asking price. On the tiny porch he discovered Miranda, wearing her customary cutoffs and half-shirt.

"Why won't you show the modern films?" she asked. The scent of whiskey wafted from her curling lips. "Why do you insist on showing movies no one wants to see?"

"Does Neil know you're here?"

She shrugged. "Neil does not own me."

Trevor seized her scabrous arms near the shoulders. She smelled like the desert. Making love to the Elephant Girl was like going to bed with a belt sander. Marvelously painful. Trevor wished that her warm, moist interior were as desiccated as her exterior, that her mouth and vagina would abrade him like the skin of her chest and legs. Cassie had been as pliable as room-temperature butter, and she'd smelled of new-mown hay. After Josh's diagnosis, she'd started slinking around Trevor, dim and silent as a shade. When the time came, she announced that she would school Josh at home. Trevor was both relieved and ashamed of his relief. "I know kids can be cruel," he said, "but the boy doesn't have long. Should we really isolate him further?" Cassie bared her teeth. She slapped her husband's face. She moved her things into Josh's room, sleeping in the extra twin bed. From then on, Trevor caught only glimpses of his wife. Impressions of her. She spent nearly every moment with their son, but Trevor knew nothing of what she taught him.

"I know how to make a business turn a profit," he said to Miranda, as they lay sidewise across his iron bed. "That's not what I'm after."

"What are you after?"

"I don't exactly know."

She placed a coarse palm against each of his cheeks. "You think you know pain," she said. "I see this. Something claws at your insides. But listen to me, Mr. Trevor. Pain is skin so dry it cracks when you smile. And you don't know shit about it."

The following evening, a small crowd of teenagers showed up at the Big Top around ten p.m. *Key Largo* had started at nine. They parked their cars in front of the screen but didn't remain in them. They got out and swarmed the concession stand. Bought popcorn and Sugar Babies, nachos and sodas from Miranda and Gina the Giantess. Rather than returning to their cars, the kids settled on the pavement. They sat munching and slurping, pushing hair out of their faces, watching Miranda and Gina talk with Sheila and Shirley and Julius, who carried legless Ruby in his arms. Just for fun, Bertram started juggling, and Duane ate popcorn with his feet. The teenagers applauded. They tossed coins, which clanked loudly against the concrete.

Trevor and Josh saw the Grand Canyon and Mount Rushmore. The World's Largest Ball of Twine and Little Bighorn Battlefield. They explored deserted mining camps and ghost towns of the Wild West. The geographic pictograms on their backs grew, filling out, moving toward completion. They ate at greasy spoons and bar-b-q restaurants, hot dog stands and hamburger joints. They stayed in motor lodges, motor courts, motor inns. Even when he grew exhausted, which happened more and more often, Josh emitted a steady stream of commentary, speaking in a breathy rush, not only to Trevor but to anyone in earshot—vacationing families, truckers, melancholy drifters. Trevor had never seen the boy so animated. His conversations weren't the stilted exchanges one might expect between strangers and a kid who's spent his life in solitary. Josh was achingly genuine. He tore at Trevor's heart.

Occasionally, someone would ask, "Is that a kid or an old man?"

"He's my son," Trevor would reply.

"What's wrong with him?"

"Nothing," Trevor would say, or "I don't know what you mean." "He has a degenerative condition" or "It's just that he's going to die soon."

As they cruised the Vegas Strip, sliding past the Tropicana and the Stardust and Circus Circus, Trevor sneaked glances at the colored lights playing over his son's crumpled face. Josh kept coughing, but he was grinning like a madman. In Oregon, Trevor took him to a shaky, bandy-legged MD, who said the time had come to make the boy comfortable. Trevor had to practically force the pain pills down his son's throat. As they crossed the border into California, Trevor and Josh cheered, high-fived.

"How will we find her?" Josh asked at a diner outside Cupertino.

"I don't know," Trevor said, eating french fries the boy had drowned in ketchup. "I don't know if she's here."

Josh's wrinkled brow furrowed further. "Why did we come?"

"I thought you should see it," Trevor said, his hands rising from the Formica tabletop to carve a sphere in the air.

In Los Angeles, they visited Universal Studios and the back lots at MGM. They toured the La Brea Tar Pits. They took off their shoes, cuffed their trousers, and strolled along the beach. They scurried into the surf, dashing back as the tide chased them in. Trevor watched the sun's light diffusing softly, flowing around dunes and seagrass and sidestepping crabs, illuminating Josh with an impossible halo, one that made him look like a holy relic, a shriveled Buddha. Trevor couldn't stop crying. He wanted to take his son's hand and walk into the ocean, to keep walking, just the two of them, to tromp all over the seafloor, to find sunken ships stuffed with pirate booty, to commune with dolphins, tiger sharks, killer whales.

"Don't worry, Dad," Josh said. "I never believed it."

"What?"

"That I'd be OK."

"What else did she tell you?"

"That no one can hold a candle to Gene Kelly."

"What else?"

"She said you know how to bring things back to life."

"You believe that?"

Josh didn't respond. He slipped his cold hand into Trevor's.

They'd almost reached the Georgia border when Trevor tried to rouse his son and found that he was unable. He pulled off the road and parked on the shoulder. He studied Joshua, who lay across the front seat as though lost in slumber, his heavy head resting on Trevor's thigh. Trevor slid out from under the boy, stepped from the car. He staggered along the gravel edge of the highway, blinded. Pontiacs and Fords and Buicks whizzed past. Horns honked. The quality of the light knocked him off balance. The sun burned unbearably, like a thousand-watt bulb without a shade. Trevor shielded his eyes with both hands. He stumbled, falling to his knees. Motorists rolled down their windows and shouted.

An older couple pulled over. The man caught Trevor under the arms and eased him toward their convertible sedan. He opened the back door, sat Trevor down on cream-colored leather, handed him a clean, pressed handkerchief. Trevor mopped his brow and cheeks. The couple looked at him with concern. He told them about Josh. Everything. From the beginning. He started with the day his son was born, with the way the light in the maternity ward had coiled itself around the boy, illuminating his particular serenity. Even as an infant, Josh had rarely wept. There had been no fixing him, no way to understand his pain. Trevor envied Cassie her ability to deny. He wondered if, wherever she was, she sensed the shift in the natural order of things. If she noticed the way Joshua's passing had altered the sun.

"I wish you could have met him," he said to the couple. "I'm not sure how I'll go on."

He wrote to Cassie's parents. They flew in from Michigan, but there was no sign of Cassie. On the day of Josh's funeral, the U.S. map etched across the boy's back was nearly complete. Trevor drove down to Florida and had the Sunshine State's blue shape added to his own map. On the way home, twenty miles south of Atlanta, he passed the decrepit remains of the Big Top Drive-In. He pulled over. He studied the sagging screen and the listing concession stand—landmarks that, like his son, had aged before their time. He thought of the bright spots of boyhood: Gary Cooper in *The Pride of the Yankees*; Margaret O'Brien in *Little Women*. Characters who faced death with a stoicism that had once struck him as pure fantasy. Trevor wanted to cry, but he was out of tears.

Less than a month after the first gawking crowd of teenagers showed up, the drive-in was crawling with customers. Not just high school kids but their parents and grandparents, their younger brothers and sisters. Whole families. Out-of-town guests. People came from Atlanta, and then they started coming from Savannah, from Charleston. Neil projected movies onto the screen, but this wasn't what drew the crowds. Most nights every spot was taken; overflow customers parked in a nearby field and walked over. They milled between cars and around the periphery. Many brought blankets and picnic baskets. On a stage Trevor and Neil had erected in front of the screen, those employees who weren't busy serving popcorn, pouring sodas, or tearing tickets did what they did best. Put their perverted bodies on display. Showcased that which set them apart. Miranda roared and stomped her scaly feet. Ruby walked on her hands. Shirley and Sheila sang duets, songs straight from the heart. Bertram performed feats of magic, making his parasitic twin disappear and reappear. Customers thronged the stage and the concession stand. It was all the employees could do to keep up. Money started pouring in. Trevor kept only enough to maintain the facilities and equipment. The rest he divided evenly among his employees.

"Mr. Trevor," Miranda said as she mounted him in his rickety bed, as they bobbed together like buoys on the swelling surface of the sea, she sliding her abrasive skin across his, "how can we ever repay you?"

On a bright fall day, they stood together outside a silver trailer that housed an Atlanta tattoo parlor. "You do realize the pain will be only temporary?" Miranda said.

"Which is worse," Trevor said, "pain or humiliation?"

The Elephant Girl laughed. She shook her head. "I cannot say. These have been bound together since I was a child. What I find most unbearable is indifference."

Four six-hour sessions were required to coat Trevor's skin in tattoos that simulated Miranda's gray scales. He'd never planned to convert his business into a carnival sideshow, but the progression had been inevitable. This is what Trevor told the reporter from the *Atlanta Star* who came out to do a feature. After a photographer snapped photos of Trevor and his employees artfully arranged on the stage, Trevor and the reporter retired to Trevor's office. The man's tie fluttered in the box fan's sticky breeze.

"This place was dead," he said. "Like Lazarus."

Trevor shook his head. "Not dead," he said, "just sleeping."

Miranda and Trevor billed themselves as the Elephant Couple. Trevor relished taking the stage with her night after night, drinking from the sea of emotions that flowed from the audience to lap at his tattooed feet—delight and horror, pity and shame. When he turned to the screen, exposing his backside, and stood gazing up at twenty feet of Marlene Dietrich or Tyrone Power, a whispering rush sounded, a collective intake of breath followed by a weighty silence. As the crowd gaped at his geographic hieroglyphs, at the forty-eight continental United States spattered in varying shades of blue across prickling human flesh, he swiveled his head toward Miranda, who smiled, lowering her scaly lids. The Elephant Girl's belly swelled, its skin taut and crackling with life, and Trevor's fingers trembled, aching to stroke its splintered surface.

Insight

We were born on the same day, in the same wing of the same charity hospital. Expelled from the same careless womb. Cut from the same checkered cloth. We look like him—share his weak chin and frizzled locks—but you don't know this because I am your eyes, and I shield you from her resentful gaze. She drinks, and she sells cigarettes and lottery tickets at a rest stop on Route 29, and as penance for wishing she'd had us, twin fruits of her loins, ousted from her body, she lets all the filthiest truckers have her. In the showers stocked with antibacterial soap that doubles as shampoo. In the cabs of their rigs. In the creaky brass bed separated from ours by one whisper-thin wall. I tell you untruths about the noises they make, say they're the sounds of irradiated luna moths throwing a celebration, of monster trucks mud wrestling. You're in no position to question, for all you know is what I've seen. Since we learned on the same day to converse in complete sentences, I've been playing the role of Narrator. Hands clasped, we move through life—two-headed, four-legged, two-eyed monster—and I describe what I see, or more accurately what I wish I saw. *We're beautiful,* I say, *and our upbringing has been perfectly normal.* In her youth she was promising with pen and ink, dreamed of being an illustrator, and through a masochistic medley of begging and scrimping, secures for us lessons in the visual arts. Tonight we sit before raw brown lumps of clay. A braless instructor paces the Community Art Center pottery studio, exhorting us to meditate on our favorite vision, locate its central truth, capture it in clay. As wet earth oozes between our fingers, I speak to you of elephants masquerading as mastodons. Of wheat-covered plains teeming with miniature ponies. She's always late, and after class, when the other students have gone home to some measure of warmth and comfort, I tug your hand, pull you behind the building, up a small incline. We settle atop a low brick wall from which the screen of a nearby XXX drive-in can be seen. One woman, two men, one in front, one behind. Electricity branches through me like a lightning strike, hardening my nipples, dampening my underpants. *What is it?* you say. *Luna moth party,* I respond. *Come on,* you say, *tell me the truth for once,* and when I turn my head, your sightless eyes seem fixed on mine. You lean in, kiss me with excruciating tenderness. Something flutters against my denim-covered crotch, but I don't know if those are your fingers, still stinking of wet clay, or my own. Ten minutes later, we sit in the back of her rusty Dodge hatchback, Rumple Minze and Old Spice fumes breaking over us like waves. *What did you girls make?* she says. *Something pretty?* I study her eyes in the rearview, the same dead eyes she passed on to us. I lift a hand, pass it in front of yours, search your face for a twitch, a tell, some indication that you see more than I imagine, but your expression remains blank as water. I drop my hand, and you seize it, clasp it to your heart. Tell her my ashtray was the best in the class. *It was,* you say, *the most beautiful thing I've never seen.*

Call Me Dixon

Dr. Slazenger's sleek, dark head is nearly always slightly cocked. Her lipstick is redder than the blood-tinged sputum that Jerry, who works noisily at the carrel next to mine, coughs into dingy, off-white handkerchiefs all the livelong day. It is Jerry's misfortune to have contracted some illness while serving in the Pacific theater, a condition that seems to me permanent, communicable, terminal. Please don't misunderstand; I have no medical training on which to base this assumption. It simply strikes me as true. Jerry, however, assures me he's going to be fine. He says he's never, in his thirty-nine years, felt better. "Soon as I get back to Jersey," he says, "I'm gonna find me a woman, someone dark and leggy like that Slazenger. Gonna take her down to the Shore and give it to her in the sand. Fuck her cross-eyed." When Jerry says such things, I nod politely and smile, the way I've decided a real Brit would. Besides, I figure it's my human obligation to humor a dying man, even if, in his ravings, he drags the pristine image of Louise Slazenger through the muck, even if his words spark tiny flames of rage within me, make boiled blood crash against my eardrums.

"You know there's nothing physically wrong with Jerry," Dr. Slazenger said three days ago, when she visited my carrel. She settled her hindquarters on the edge of my desk and sat, one patent leather pump planted on the ground, the other dangling from the tip of a narrow, stockinged foot. "You know the illness is all in his mind."

Dr. Slazenger is my direct superior. The filterless Dunhills she chain smokes deposit flecks of tobacco on her tongue. Each time she plucks a brown shred from her mouth in my presence, I consider asking for it. I've thought of mixing specks of Slazenger-saliva-soaked tobacco with dried herbs and flowers, making sachets of them, tulle-wrapped bundles designed to freshen sock drawers and other hidden places.

"Did you hear me, Dixon?"

"What about the blood?" I said.

"Blood?"

"On Jerry's handkerchiefs. The blood."

Dr. Slazenger uncrossed and recrossed her long legs, shifting her weight from one cheek to the other. I thought I heard her white coat crackle. "Don't be an ass, Gene," she said. "You know there's no blood."

My name isn't actually Eugene Dixon. Dixon was an Englishman I discovered swinging from a heating pipe on the fourth floor of a flophouse in London's blitzed-out East End. This was three months ago. Three months earlier I'd abandoned a USO tour of North Africa, stowed away aboard a merchantman bound for London, taken a job in this fleabag hotel—one of only three buildings on its block the Luftwaffe had left standing. Dixon's swaying corpse was outfitted in gray wool trousers and a houndstooth sport coat. Before climbing onto the rickety Queen Anne chair I found upended beneath his dangling wingtips, he'd removed his navy-and-maroon-striped necktie and folded it into a neat square. I discerned from the dark patch on Dixon's trousers front that he'd pissed himself, smelled the fecal matter filling his underpants. My first instinct was to right the chair, climb up, use my penknife to saw through the braided leather ligature wound round the pipe and Dixon's bruised neck, lower his lids over his fixed, bulging eyes—maybe even use his handkerchief to push the swollen tongue behind the barrier of his blue lips. Before I could do any of these things, however, I spied the trifolded note on the desktop. I read the note, opened the attaché case I found on the floor. Discovered Dixon's secrets: encoded audiotapes and documents entrusted to his keeping; a code he'd only just the night before, in the close, gamy air of this room, managed to crack. Yellowing, still faintly gardenia-scented letters from a childhood sweetheart, a girl named Louise Slazenger.

"You're taller than I imagined," Dr. Slazenger said, when she greeted me at the front door of the manor house at Paisley Park, fifty miles northwest of London. This estate, now known as Station P, was quietly purchased by British intelligence four years ago, in 1939, and converted into a clandestine, state-of-the-art decryption base. As I crossed the threshold, the mansion, in whose schizophrenic structure Gothic, Baroque, and Tudor styles dogfought for dominance, seemed to swallow me whole. "And not nearly as savage."

After earning a linguistics doctorate from Cambridge, the actual Eugene Dixon fled his homeland, spending the last twelve of his thirty-seven years in the States, living on a Navajo reservation in New Mexico, studying the ancient language of the *Dine,* which simply translates to "the people." This tongue is unwritten, but in Dixon's suitcase I discovered notebooks in which he'd attempted to set down phonetically the components of the dialect. After cutting free his corpse, I followed the instructions Dixon had laid out in his farewell. Bathed and anointed his skin with strong-smelling unctions I found in his Dopp kit. Dressed him in the deerskin breechcloth and hip leggings I discovered among his possessions. The moccasins, the silver concho belt, the rabbit-fur cloak. Dixon's body was sun-bronzed, and the curved pieces of turquoise I dug out of his suitcase fit snugly into his pierced earlobes. His hair was shorter on the sides, where it had at one time been shaved to the skin with the flat of a pre-Columbian flint knife.

"I heard you'd gone native," said Louise Slazenger.

"Yes, well," I said, watching her pluck tobacco from the tip of her tongue, "you can't believe everything you hear."

She led me past sitting rooms, drawing rooms, bedrooms, all crowded with desks, transmitters, telephones, headsets, voluminous spools of wire, receivers, coffin-size calculating machines, typewriters, phonographs, men in shirtsleeves with slicked hair, women in loose trousers with soft curls. The station crackled with a dull, irrepressible hum, one that seemed to animate the assembled players, jerking them about like marionettes. The steady stream of vital chatter was like an electrical current, and as I watched Dr. Slazenger's body sway a few steps ahead of mine—anomalous white coat, unbearably straight stocking seams—this hum filled me, keying me up, setting my teeth on edge, my heart aflame.

It was the letters Louise Slazenger had written Gene Dixon as a girl of fourteen, not the fact that Dixon and I had the same build and the same amount of medium brown hair remaining, not the fact that the Germans were still sporadically bombing London's East End, that had convinced me to adopt Dixon's persona, to pore over every scrap in his suitcase and pockets, to glean as much as I could, to pull out and tweak the accent I'd perfected while touring, for nine seasons, with the road company of the Illinois Shakespeare Theater, where my Iago routinely brought down the house. Dr. Slazenger's girlhood missives were lyrical, evocative, heart-wrenching—nothing like the letter she'd written Dixon two months earlier, inviting him to join the decryption team at Station P—and as I followed her up the main staircase to the third floor, padding over carpets that swallowed the barest hint of footfall, I searched in vain for some sign of that fresh, unfettered author.

"I can't believe you took your degree in statistics," I said. "You should be writing novels. Verse. Plays, perhaps."

Dr. Slazenger smiled mirthlessly. "I see you haven't lost your sense of humor."

A tall oak door swung inward and on the other side I discovered Dr. Max Tungsten—chess champion, crossword fiend, and director of Station P—and Jerry Clifton, the American code breaker with whom Drs. Tungsten and Slazenger had decided to partner me. Or rather, with whom they'd decided to partner Eugene Dixon.

"Glad to know you, Gene," said Jerry, extending a tremulous hand. The other hand remained in his lap, balled around a handkerchief on which I thought I spied a pink blush. "They tell me you've spent a dozen years with the *Dine*."

Turns out Jerry was raised by a nanny, a Choctaw named Mikahala, who fled the Mississippi reservation on which she'd been born, making her way north to New Jersey in search of a better life. As soon as little Jerry began to babble, Mikahala had started teaching him her native tongue; as a result, he spoke the language fluently. Jerry had served the US Navy as a code talker in the Pacific theater for nearly a year before he came down with his mysterious illness, one no doctor had been able to diagnose.

"You two should make quite a team," Dr. Slazenger said as she showed Jerry and me to the third-floor library and our neighboring carrels. "And remember: the fate of the free world is in your hands."

Louise Slazenger's use of such platitudinous phrases seems to me a deliberate effort to mask her intelligence, her precise grasp of the human condition. I haven't yet determined why she is so modest. Brilliant women make many men nervous, but I can't imagine Louise letting that get to her, giving in to some testosterone-inspired preference for the yielding, the kittenish, the demure. I've tried asking her about this, but it seems that Jerry is always standing in my way—bludgeoning Dr. Slazenger with his broad, ham-fisted humor, jokes at which she giggles politely, not wanting, I believe, to harm the man's feelings. Two nights ago, as my fellows at Station P—mathematicians, linguists, puzzle freaks—drank black lager and dandelion wine, fox-trotting and Lindy Hopping around Paisley Park's grand ballroom as they loosened up, letting swing music and fermented beverages carry them like swiftly flowing streams far from rationing and twelve-hour workdays, far from sleepless nights and air raids, far from limbless veterans and thoughts of what might, at that moment, be happening to deployed loved ones, as our collective consciousness concocted a dream other than the one we're living, an alternate reality, one in which the World has not yet conceived of War, I stood in a corner, watching Jerry drag poor Louise Slazenger around the dance floor. I don't usually imbibe, but even I was having a glass of sherry, embracing rather than fighting the droning hum that threads through each of us, weaving us together, binding us as tightly as the cord with which the real Eugene Dixon ended his life.

When the sight of Jerry and Dr. Slazenger dancing began to turn my stomach, when I felt the flush of intoxication stealing across my face, I let myself out through one of the ballroom's X-taped French doors. Shoving my hands deep into Gene Dixon's pockets, fingering the items I found there—shillings and ha'pennies, a black rabbit's foot, my own penknife, a gold cigarette lighter—I meandered through the gardens. It's just June, but lately the atmosphere in Buckinghamshire has been steamy, reminding me of the South Side of Chicago at summer's height, and I peeled off Dixon's second-best sport coat. Thanks to the war, Paisley Park's gardens are overgrown, unkempt, but there's a beauty to them, a shaggy, weedy elegance, something no amount of bombing or terror or neglect could obliterate.

I stood on a gentle rise, gazing across the grounds. I fogged my eyes, trying to envision the plateaus of the American Southwest—a part of my own nation I've never seen. I imagined huntsmen on horseback, driving frothing palominos into striated canyons, plunging through knee-high succulents and scrubs. I saw Eugene Dixon among them—lean, ropy, clad in leggings and breechcloth, dark hair flowing behind him, a native cry on his lips. He would have known instantly whether the pregnant moon hanging over Station P was dilating or contracting, and I felt myself straining, with all my might, toward Dixondom.

"Dixon? Is that you?"

Jerry Clifton, who'd apparently decided to give poor Dr. Slazenger a break, appeared beside me. He dropped a hand on my shoulder. The damp heat of his palm leached through Gene Dixon's woven cotton shirt and I fought the urge to shudder. He was soaked, was Jerry—damp underarm rings, splotched back and chest. I could only imagine the state of the area between his thighs, could only imagine the distress in which Louise Slazenger must have found herself—trapped in his embrace, forced against his bizarre, barrel-shaped body, his distended abdomen and concave chest. And there, as if on cue—the hacking. Out came a handkerchief. Once Jerry's fit had peaked and receded, I glanced at the dingy cloth in his left hand. I thought of Dr. Slazenger sitting on my desk, her white coat crackling, and tried to convince myself that the handkerchief's bloodred aspect was merely a trick of the moonlight.

"As a kid," Jerry said, "whenever I'd ask Mikahala about the moon, she'd slap my face. *Never speak of the moon,* she'd say. *Ask me only about the sun.* She told me the Choctaw worship

Hushtali, the sun. They see it as a deity, believe it gives and takes life. Believe Fire, the sun's direct representative, possesses an intelligence all its own."

As is often the case when we sit at our carrels, bent to the task set for us by Drs. Tungsten and Slazenger—that task being the breaking of the code Eugene Dixon cracked some three months ago, the night before he hanged himself—I felt the distinct and cumbersome weight of Jerry's gaze. I often suspect that, when it comes to me and my story, Jerry is beset by doubts. That he harbors more than a passing suspicion that I am not, in fact, Gene Dixon, English expatriate, polyglot, code breaker, and honorary Navajo. Please don't misunderstand; Jerry has never expressed anything like this in my presence, nor have I caught the barest whiff of such a rumor circulating amongst our fellow cryptographers. It's probably just paranoia. *But what reason has Jerry Clifton,* I asked myself as I let my gaze traipse over weed-choked hollyhocks, bluebells, and tulips, all soaked silver in the sheen of the pregnant moon, *to speak to me of the godlike and intelligent aspects of fire?*

"Want to know something crazy?" I said. "My brother was also named Jerry."

"No shit?"

"No shit."

"What happened?"

"He died."

"How?"

"Tuberculosis. When we were kids."

Jerry Clifton wheezed. "Jeez, Gene," he said. "I'm awfully sorry to hear that."

When she'd had enough laudanum to feel euphoric but not yet enough to start nodding out, my mother used to say the only thing that stands between man and madness is his ability to dream. She preferred fictions to the reality of life, and she instilled the same preference in me. As a boy I would watch her mutate, with the aid of a little greasepaint, a veil, a flimsy accent, from two-bit stage actress and lapsed Catholic into Goneril, Kate, Mistress Quickly, Lady Macbeth. My mother was happy to adopt the persona of anyone, anyone at all, other than herself, and she possessed an abiding belief in one's ability to change. "You can be anyone or anything," she would say. "Never let people tell you different." I longed to believe her, and I tried then, as I am trying now, to convince myself that she was on to something. That in spite of the base circumstances in which I was raised, in spite of the setbacks I've faced, in spite of my own destructive tendencies, there's hope for me yet. That I'm not necessarily stuck with myself. I've spent my adult life following my mother, treading the boards, changing outward aspects as easily and as often as I change my clothes. She was the most convincing liar I ever knew, and in this, too, I follow her.

Why, then, I asked myself as I lay in the dormitory listening to Jerry Clifton cough and sputter in the twin bed next to mine, *had I blurted out what I'd blurted out to him?* For it had been my own brother, not Eugene Dixon's, who'd died of tuberculosis at fifteen. Who'd spent his final, fevered, bedridden days poring over his battered copy of the Vulgate of Jerome, the saint for whom he was named, committing parables to memory, mumbling Latin orisons, rubbing his whispering palms together. Violent coughing fits left my brother deflated, cast a spectral pallor over his skin. Jerry clutched always in one hand a handkerchief with which he covered his mouth—a cloth that, as the day wore on, became increasingly soaked with blood. I can still see my mother, standing over a soapy sinkful of these pink cloths in dawn's light, scrubbing, mumbling, "Out, out."

After a night of tossing, I sat in the dining hall, eating crumpets with marmalade and bangers, drinking Assam tea, perusing the *Times,* fretting about Jerry Clifton, who could, with just a spot of detective work, find out that Eugene had had no brothers. That Reginald and Celeste Dixon had had, aside from Gene, only one daughter, Amelia, a sweet, guileless girl who suffered intermittently from hysterical blindness and had lost her life when she'd rushed, at nineteen, into a burning barn to save a litter of feral kittens she'd stashed there for safekeeping.

Paisley Park's dining room has been converted into a mess for the statisticians, philologists, mathematicians, and support personnel—a group that seems to be growing by the hour. Everywhere I look, I spy a face I've never seen before. But I digress. The *Times* was full of the usual reports: intensified petrol rationing, the recent surrender of Axis forces in North Africa, the sinking of an American destroyer near Java, speculation on Churchill's next move. I was finishing up an article buried in the Metro section, a piece on an unsolved, and, in light of the current global crisis, largely ignored, three-month-old case of arson—a blaze had devoured an East End residential hotel, one of the only such buildings the Blitz had left standing—when a throat was cleared prettily beside me, when I looked up and into the flowerlike face of Claire Swift.

"Anything worth noting?" she said.

I should probably point out that Claire and I have been carrying on a love affair, one I have every intention of ending. This excitable girl, a stenographer and aspiring actress, shares not only my passion for Shakespeare but also my tendency to insomnia, and when we chanced upon one another in the first-floor library two months ago at three a.m. we fell immediately and without a thought for consequences into one another's arms. I have no idea how much time passed between the real Dixon's last sexual experience and his death, but I myself hadn't made love in better than a year and had been so tormented by my desire for Louise Slazenger that when Claire—unlike Dr. Slazenger, a fragile, willowy blond—laid her little hand upon my wrist, I lost all control. Claire often asks about my life in the States, or rather about Gene Dixon's life in the States, and when we make love, she begs me to play the part of the Navajo warrior. Thanks to her, I've crafted a whole hatful of fictitious but perfectly plausible tales about the daily lives of the *Dine.*

"The usual," I said, in response to Claire's query, folding the *Times* and tossing it aside as she settled close to me on the bench. Sultry, humid air drifted in through the windows, and Claire's thin dress clung to her skin. "What about on your end? Anything to report?"

She nodded. "Something major. It seems there's a spy in our midst."

Rumor has it that one of our cohort at Paisley Park has been leaking secrets to the Jerrys, who of late have been cracking our codes faster than we can formulate them. This doesn't come as much of a shock to me, since, as I've mentioned, the staff at Station P is growing exponentially; with so many people milling about, a leak or two seems unavoidable. When I pointed this out to Claire, however, she shook her pretty blond head and said the information that's being handed off is quite carefully guarded. Only top brass have access. Consensus is that the spy is one of Station P's directors. Then she leaned in and told me where *her* suspicions pointed.

"But it's unthinkable," I said. "Louise Slazenger is devoted to the Allied cause."

"Or so she'd like us to think," said Claire, who got quite cross the time I inadvertently whimpered Dr. Slazenger's name at the moment of orgasm. "But I'd wager a month's pay that the good doctor has a skeleton or two in her cupboard."

I spent the morning in my carrel, my nose to the ostensible grindstone. Thanks to Dixon, I possess the key to the code Jerry Clifton and I have been assigned to break, and when the time is right, I will reveal it and reap the rewards. Meanwhile, when I'm purportedly code cracking, I instead pore over the letters Louise Slazenger wrote as a girl—letters Dixon clearly cherished, letters he carried better than five thousand miles, to the southwestern U.S. and back to his foggy homeland—and the volumes I've plucked from the shelves of Paisley Park's libraries. These consist, mainly, of the works of Shakespeare, to whose rapier wordplay and profound grasp of the human condition I was introduced at five, when my mother had me portray a rotating cast of fairies—Peaseblossom, Mustardseed, et al.—to her Queen Titania in the *Dream*. What hours I don't while away on twenty-year-old letters and iambic pentameter are spent earnestly attempting to teach myself the Navajo language using the phonetic notes Dixon so magnanimously provided.

It was to this task that, after disentangling myself from Claire Swift in the dining hall, I was devoting my partial attention, the other part being occupied by thoughts of Dr. Slazenger's sleek, dark head, of her fingers plucking tobacco from her pink tongue, of whether she might, in fact, be operating as a double agent for the Jerrys, when comprehension broke over me like a raw egg. It was the sort of knowledge one glimpses only when one is lost in thought on two disparate subjects, disconnected, as it were, in a state that allows the mind to make bounding, free-associative leaps. I suddenly knew, with utter certainty, that Dixon's notebooks contain more than phonetic representations of the Navajo language. That buried within them is a message. A message, unbelievable as this sounds, intended specifically for me.

On one of his notebook pages, Dixon had penned an encoded notice he'd hoped the person who found his remains and carried out his wishes for their disposal—that person being me—would labor over and eventually decipher. The information has to do only metaphorically with why Dixon took his life, the immediate, concrete reasons for which were elucidated in his farewell note. It has more to do with the human animal and his conception of self, of what it means to be *I* or *you* or *he* or *we*. The implications of Dixon's hidden communiqué struck terror into my heart, which began to pound. My hands trembled, and my skin, already damp from the heat, grew slick with perspiration. When a hand fell upon my shoulder, I shrieked, whirled in my chair, and found Jerry Clifton hovering over my carrel.

"Dixon?" he said. "You look like you've seen the devil."

I wiped my palms on Gene Dixon's wool trousers, tried to slow the rapid flutter of my heart. "Nonsense," I said. "I'm right as rain."

"Slazenger's the mole," Jerry said, lowering his voice. "I'm telling you. I knew she was a minx from the jump. Those tits, that ass, the way she parades around. I said to myself, here's a girl who gets up to no good."

"I don't know," I said. "Where's the proof?"

"Very few people have access to all the codes. Mark my words, Gene . . ."

"But she's always struck me as so high-minded. So sincere."

"High-minded?" Jerry's snort turned into a chortle, which progressed into a series of racking coughs. He pulled a handkerchief from his pocket, wiped red-flecked saliva from his lips. "You've obviously never danced with her."

It's true that I've never danced with Dr. Slazenger; the same, however, could not be said of the real Gene Dixon. *Village dances will never be the same without you,* Louise lamented in a letter she posted after Dixon's parents packed up their possessions and fled their Somerset farm for the wilds of Northumberland. Three months earlier, a rotting barn that straddled the property line between the Dixons' farm and the Slazengers' had gone up in flames, killing Amelia Dixon and seven black-and-white kittens. This was the barn to whose loft Louise and Gene, as hormonal adolescents—monstrous, half-formed creatures standing one foot in the cradle, the other in the grave—would retire after village dances; here they would peel away one another's clothing like candy wrappers or fruit skins, explore taut pubescent flesh, cross barriers erected by church, family, state. *You know I never wished poor Amelia any harm,* Louise wrote in one of her missives, *but even now, I regret nothing. How were we supposed to know that those were her foundlings, or that she would come running? I remember only clasping hands, dropping to our knees, so close to the inferno we felt it licking our skin. She had no business there. That fire was a prayer, and it was* ours. *Please write, Gene. Tell me you understand. Tell me this is a real fever that burns me, not one I've only dreamed up.*

"You all right, old man?" I said to Jerry, whose balled handkerchief, I swear to God, was raining red droplets onto the lilac carpet. "When was the last time you saw a doctor?"

"Yesterday." Jerry nodded rather sagely. "He says I'm fit as a fiddle."

No physician ever said that of my brother Jerry, whose greatest fear, as he drew near his end, became the unquenchable fires of hell. It was that damned copy of the Vulgate of Saint Jerome my mother gave him as a lark when he was only six and still untouched by the consumption that would steal his young life. She never imagined that he would teach himself Latin and end up reading the volume repeatedly, that an obsession with the rites of the Roman church would possess Jerry like a demon neither she nor I would be able to exorcise. Once,

I hid my brother's Vulgate and tried to engage him instead with reading material I enjoyed, the works of Shakespeare and other masters of the dramatic form—Sophocles, Ben Jonson, Henrik Ibsen, Oscar Wilde. This boy, who was doomed by age twelve, who had every reason to lose himself in a fictional dreamworld, insisted on facing reality head-on. Jerry wept and howled until I caved. "You should've held firm," my mother said. "Doctrine will bring him nothing but sorrow." "It's his only comfort," I replied. "Like laudanum, in book form."

Our mother never understood either of us. Just as she never understood our fathers, a couple of cut-rate actors who romanced, impregnated, and abandoned her. It was the pain that plagued her after our difficult births—first mine, and then, only eleven months later, my brother's—that turned her to laudanum in the first place, and though she never said it, I knew she blamed us for her dependence. A bottle of the dark, sweet-smelling liquid was forever stashed under our kitchen sink, and as Jerry's illness progressed, our mother's habit grew. "How can one be expected to sleep," she would whimper as the two of us sat at the wobbly kitchen table, running lines for a second-rate production of *Twelfth Night* or *The Taming of the Shrew,* listening to my brother hack and rattle, "or to keep their wits about them, in the midst of such a racket?"

"She wants me dead," Jerry said to me, one month before the end.

"Don't be ridiculous."

"It won't be long."

"Don't talk like that."

"I need you to do something for me. To make me a promise."

When my brother asked me to administer last rites, I pointed out that I was no priest, but he said this didn't matter. We knew no priests, and in Jerry's desperate reckoning, I was the obvious choice. I needed only to procure some olive oil, bless it according to the sacraments, memorize the words I would speak as I anointed him in six places: eyelids, ears, nostrils, lips, hands, feet. *By this holy unction and his own most gracious mercy, may the Lord pardon you whatever sin you have committed by sight, by hearing, by smell, by taste and speech, by touch, by ability to walk.* My brother had committed no sins—he'd never had the chance—but when I pointed this out, Jerry just shook his head.

"We're all sinners," he said. "We're born that way."

"How can you believe in things you've never seen?"

"I've never seen the ocean," said Jerry, "but I believe in it. Same goes for China. And love. How could anyone spend more than a minute on this planet and not believe in love?"

One month later, I came home from school on a Wednesday to find Jerry's bed empty, his sheets and pillows burned to ashes. Our mother sat at the kitchen table, sobbing, but I'd seen enough of her performances to know when she was acting.

"What happened?" I said.

"He slipped away."

"Where is he?"

"The crematorium."

Someone had put quite a dent in the laudanum under the sink, and she was sober, something I'd learned by that late date to discern without question.

"Shrew," I said, and slapped her face.

"What's wrong with you?"

"Not me." I spun, hurled the bottle against the rose and lilac wallpaper. The glass exploded. Brown liquid splattered outward like the rays of the sun. I turned back to my mother, who was on her feet, both hands pressed to her mouth, watching her succor seep to the floor, crying honest-to-goodness tears. "It's not what's wrong with me."

I wasn't quite sixteen, but that night I fled the house in which I was born, never to return. I took only three things with me: the vial of olive oil we'd blessed, my brother and I; Jerry's battered copy of the Vulgate of Saint Jerome; and the insatiable desire to provide some poor soul with a measure of relief.

Very early this morning, once again bedeviled by visions of my brother roasting in eternal flames, I rose from bed and roamed the corridors of Paisley Park. Thanks to blackout curtains, the inky darkness is impenetrable, but I can manage the route from the men's dormitory to the third-floor library sightless—as blind as poor gouged Gloucester. The air in Station P was particularly stifling this morning, and I longed to tear the curtains aside, throw open the windows, usher in the predawn air. I mounted the stairs, counting fifty-seven steps, padded barefoot over thick carpets. Discovered a light spilling across the hallway. Found the library door ajar.

Louise Slazenger stood over my carrel, lit by the glow of a desk lamp, her head bent over Eugene Dixon's notebooks, over the letters she'd written as a girl of fourteen. When she caught sight of me, she plucked a packet of Dunhills from the pocket of her blue robe, pulled out a white cylinder, placed it between her lips—bloodred even now, in the dead of night. I moved forward, my hand sliding into the pocket of Gene Dixon's bathrobe, retrieving the gold lighter I'd discovered in a velvet box at the bottom of his suitcase. I flicked the wheel with my thumb, struck flint, ignited a spark. The sight of Louise Slazenger's face, lit by the small flame, stirred a memory, one that is not my own. I saw her as a girl of twelve, wearing a plaid dress, a light jacket, saddle shoes. Her hair hung in braids down her back, but even then her sleek dark head was cocked. I saw the two of us huddled together on a windy day, struggling to light our first filched cigarette.

"You've heard the rumors?" said Dr. Slazenger. She picked

up one of the letters she'd written. She made no apologies for rifling through my desk.

"I have."

Plucking a speck of tobacco from her tongue, Louise turned, paced the distance from my carrel to Jerry Clifton's. "After I took my doctorate," she said, "I spent a number of years working abroad, mainly in Austria but also, for a time, in Germany. I was a cog in the machinery of a large international accounting firm, Schmidt and Vogler. Several Englishmen worked for the firm at the same time, but I didn't socialize with them. I hardly ever left my flat. I am, as you may recall, solitary by nature."

Her words echoed the opening line of Dixon's farewell note: *Like the Phoenix, I am a solitary creature.*

"It is now being suggested," she continued, "that I am a British-born German operative who bumped off Louise Slazenger and stole her identity years ago. That I returned to this country and worked my way up with the deliberate intent of sabotaging Allied intelligence."

I'd settled on the edge of my desk, and I watched Louise turn from Jerry Clifton's carrel, toward me, and begin to glide forward. Clutching the letter, she drew close—closer than seemed appropriate. Closer than seemed advisable in light of the heat.

"I'm not the girl who wrote these letters," she said softly.

"You're not?"

She shook her head. "Just as you're not Gene Dixon."

"But I am."

Dr. Slazenger smiled. "Gene never would have come here. He would have made some grand, absurd, symbolic gesture. Slit his throat. Doused himself in kerosene, set himself ablaze in the streets. Dixon never would have quietly taken up his post, worked so diligently these last months." Louise reached up, ran a fingertip along the edge of my jaw, traced the outline of my lips. The scents of gardenia, tobacco, powder, and perspiration washed over me, weakened my knees. "I know your features better than I know my own. Know your body better than my own. More than two decades have passed since we set the blaze, since I watched your parents pack up and flee the farm, since I wrote these letters. When I received no answer, I convinced myself that I loathed you. Told myself you were entirely to blame for what happened to Amelia, for our separation. But when I look into my heart, I know that isn't true."

I can see Louise Slazenger's lovely face pressing forward, her bloodred lips touching mine, her hands caressing my cheeks, ruffling my hair. After that I can recall only fire. In our incendiary coupling there seemed to be no organs, no orifices. I can picture no penis, no mouth, no vagina, no breast. Did I sweep everything off the desk, throw her down, tear open her blue robe, split her in two? Did I lift her up, impale her on my engorged member? Did we fall to the carpet and tear into one another like animals—biting, snarling, whining, shifting positions and loci of penetration? I cannot answer these questions. It seems to me that all these things happened, and all at once. It seems that Louise Slazenger and I were relieved of our corporeal selves. That we floated above the encryption station, above the English countryside, hovered like twisting clouds of smoke, flicked like tongues of flame. When it was all over, when the haze that filled the third-floor library began to dissipate and the tactile world crept back into existence, Dr. Slazenger and I found ourselves crawling around on the carpet like a pair of infants.

"How's Claire Swift going to take this?" Louise said as we lay facing one another, passing a Dunhill back and forth.

"Hang Claire Swift."

"Tell me something." Louise lifted her head, propped it on a fist, cocked it at my favorite angle. "When you were in the States, did you locate your God of Fire?"

Like certain tribes native to the Americas, Eugene Dixon had written in the first paragraph of his farewell note, *I have always believed in the supremacy of a Sun God. Fire is the ultimate cleanser, the ultimate leveler. It destroys, but inherent in its destruction is promise. Hope. Fire burns things back to a blank slate on which anything can be written.*

"No," I said, "but I stopped looking for him a long time ago."

Louise broke down then, really began to sob, and I was seized by the sudden urge to taste her tears. I gently touched her eyelids, her ears, her nostrils, lips, hands, and feet. Said I would come to her aid later that day, when MI-5 and the Corps of Military Police would arrive to interrogate her. Said I would produce the letters she'd written for analysis against a sample of her current handwriting. That I would testify, under oath, that I'd known her since she was in diapers. Later, once Louise had stopped weeping, once she'd wrapped herself in her bathrobe and exited the library, I sat Indian style before the room's brick hearth. I reread her passionate, poetic missives, one by one, before balling them up and piling them on the grate, before using Gene Dixon's lighter to set them ablaze. Within minutes, it was as though the letters had never been written.

"I'm sorry," I said half an hour ago as I sat in Dr. Tungsten's office, sealed off from the rest of Station P by its tall oak door, facing a mustachioed captain from Special Branch and two clean-shaven CMP lieutenants. "I can't be sure."

"But you grew up with Louise Slazenger," said Dr. Tungsten.

"Yes," I said, "but my family moved from Somerset to Northumberland more than twenty years ago. The last time I saw Louise, she was fourteen."

The mustachioed captain leaned forward. "And you're unable to confirm that this woman is the girl you once knew."

When one is attempting to create a plausible fiction, the maintenance of eye contact is key. Actors and con men learn this early on. Good liars are born with the knowledge. It is true that I am all these things; however, what I said next was neither lie nor scripted sentiment, and I boldly met the gaze of the CMP lieutenants, the MI-5 captain, Dr. Tungsten. I even sought out Dr. Slazenger's gaze, but she refused to look up.

"I wish I could," I said. "I honestly do. But I cannot say with certainty that this woman is Louise Slazenger."

"What about the letters?" said one of the lieutenants.

"Letters?"

"We understood you were in possession of letters written by Dr. Slazenger that would prove her identity."

"I'm afraid there's been a misunderstanding," I said. "Any such letters I had were destroyed in a fire long ago."

As Louise was escorted away by the CMP lieutenants, she dragged her eyes up from the lilac carpet to my face. Her pupils danced like windblown drops of rain.

"I was mistaken," she said. "You *are* Gene Dixon."

In his suicide note, Dixon confessed that he'd never gotten over the death of his sister. *Louise Slazenger and I set that loft ablaze,* he wrote, *in an effort to glimpse the glowing visage of the God of Fire.* Neither Dixon nor Louise had seen this God, nor had they seen poor Amelia running into the rickety, flaming barn. Unlike the Phoenix, Amelia Dixon had never risen from the ashes, and, crippled by guilt, Gene had spent the rest of his life searching—in books on metaphysics, religion, and philosophy; in university classrooms; in the mysterious profundities of language; in the far-flung reaches of the Americas—for proof that some sort of divine intelligence is at work in our lives. Unfortunately, Dixon never found it.

But I did.

Three months before Dr. Slazenger was escorted from the grounds of Paisley Park, I stood outside a rattrap hotel in London, watching a conflagration. This was after I'd read Dixon's note, after I'd constructed—from dresser, coffee table, and the Queen Anne chairs—a makeshift pyre, after I'd laid Dixon's cleansed, anointed body across this combustible nest. After I'd doused the room with kerosene, used Dixon's lighter to spark the blaze, fled with my brother's battered Vulgate and all Gene Dixon's possessions. From an adjacent alley, I watched flames devour the dry timber. I listened to whistles, shouts, and pounding footfalls. I was staggered by the way the fire illumed the night—like a counterfeit sun, one that reveals things the actual sun cannot. At one point I closed my eyes, and when I opened them again, my heart dropped into Gene Dixon's wingtips.

"My God," I breathed.

Clearly visible through the flames, through the roiling black smoke, was a face. A colossal visage with seething eyes, gaping mouth. The Fire God's flesh twisted and crawled. His features rippled with varicolored brilliance. I stood frozen, one hand pressed to my mouth, the other clutching my brother's book. The Fire God's kaleidoscopic gaze fell upon me, and I felt it searching me, draining my power. He said my name—not my true name, but Eugene Dixon's. When I pointed out his mistake, the Fire God cackled, a sound that shook the superheated air, made the cobblestones tremble. *Never question the God of Fire,* he said. *You are Gene Dixon.* I dropped to my knees, and the Latin phrases I'd memorized years earlier rose unbidden to my lips. I touched my eyes, my ears, my nose, mouth, hands, and feet. For whom or what I was begging forgiveness, I am still not certain.

"Bad luck about Slazenger," Jerry Clifton said moments ago, as he joined me in the third-floor corridor. I'd just left Tungsten's office, seen Louise and her captors disappear past the stair's turning. "I'll miss that minx."

"Yes," I said. "A damn shame."

Jerry and I fought our way through the corridor, which was choked with people, most of whom I'd never seen. They were talking all at once, and the droning purr enveloped me, insulating me against what may or may not exist outside the walls: the war, flaming hotels, the South Side of Chicago, laudanum, the USO, tuberculosis, the Jersey Shore, a people known as the *Dine,* the American West.

"Jerry," I said. "I've got that code just about cracked."

"No shit?"

"No shit."

"When you gonna tell Tungsten?"

"Today. I thought we could tell him together."

"But I haven't helped," said Jerry. "You've broken the thing on your own."

We'd made it back to the library, and Jerry Clifton and I faced one another between our carrels. I reached out, grasped his damp shoulder. He smiled, and wine-dark blood cascaded from his lips, flowed over his chin, coursed down his white shirtfront.

"You have helped, old man," I said. "More than you know."

Jerry's run off to grab me a cup of Assam tea, and I sit now at my carrel, studying the notebooks Gene Dixon filled with phonetic representations of the Navajo language. I know now that these notebooks don't contain just one encoded message but thousands of them. Or, rather, that the markings Dixon made, in his careful, upright print, can be interpreted any number of ways. Can represent anything I want them to. Or anything *you* want them to. Or anything Winston Churchill wants them to. That this is the nature of language. Words, sentences, phrases possess meaning only as we assign it to them. Just as we have a persona only as it has been assigned us by parents, siblings, colleagues, lovers. *We are such stuff as dreams are made on,* according to Shakespeare, *and our little life is rounded with a sleep.* On one page of his notebooks, Gene Dixon seems to be saying *Each of us is doomed. True change, in terms of the human animal, the human psyche, is impossible.* On another he seems to be saying *You are the God of Fire. I am the God of Fire. Therefore, there is no God of Fire.* However, I am fully capable of reinterpreting Dixon's encoded notes, of challenging his intelligence, and the possible implications of his hidden communiqués no longer terrify me. Sitting here at my carrel, allowing the hum that fills Station P to wash over and through me, I now realize that I am all-powerful. I am the One True God, and I can honestly say that nothing frightens me.

Well, one thing. But Jerry Clifton is the only person to whom I've mentioned my brother, and Clifton will be back with my tea soon enough. We will then head over to Max Tungsten's office, announce that we've broken the code with which those damned Jerrys have been vexing the Allied cause. Dr. Tungsten will crow and clap us on the back. He'll gather the staff and make an announcement, and tonight, in the grand ballroom, there will be a celebration. Jerry Clifton will turn to me at some point, drunk on lager and whiskey, tears shimmering in his eyes, and he'll thank me for being so generous. I'll brush aside his thanks, tell him I couldn't have done it without him, for, as I may have already mentioned, I believe it is my human obligation to humor a dying man. And at some point in the coming days, when Jerry Clifton's body is discovered on the grounds of Paisley Park, his remains charred, I will have no trouble weeping.

Perhaps, once dental records from the great state of New Jersey have been procured, it will come out that the man we knew as Jerry Clifton was an impostor. That the teeth anchored in his jaw originally belonged to someone with a different name. Even if this ironic turn of events comes to pass, we will, no doubt, inter Jerry Clifton, or whoever he may be, as a hero for his contributions to the cause. I will sit on the front row of the Paisley Park chapel, holding the hand of Claire Swift, who will weep, her pretty blond head on my shoulder. When I'm asked to say a few words about my code-breaking partner, I will arrange my features into a tragic mask. I will face the teeming Station P staff—who will pack the chapel beyond capacity, who will spill from its windows and doors. I will clear my throat and say without a hint of compunction, "*I* am Gene Dixon. I *am* Gene Dixon. *I am Gene Dixon.*"

Fairy Tale Triptych

FLIGHT OF THE BUSINESSMAN

I was sitting on a toadstool eating my lunch when a businessman landed in the grass beside me. Munching nectar-on-toast, I shielded my eyes with the tip of a wing and drank him in. It was unusual to find a businessman so far from his natural habitat, especially in spring. To be perfectly honest, I'd never seen one before. If not for an Identification of Warm-Blooded Bipeds class I took at the Learning Annex, I don't think I would have been able to place him.

"Are you on a coffee break, or is this your lunch hour?" I asked, eager to use the vocabulary from my class.

The businessman picked a dandelion and blew white spores into the air. They settled on the jacket and pants of his gray flannel suit. "Neither," he said. "I quit."

"Oh." I tried with my tone to indicate that I understood the gravity of the situation. "Do you have something else lined up? Have you sent out résumés?"

The businessman shook his head. "It wasn't planned. I walked out in the middle of a board meeting. About an hour ago."

"I see."

Wrapping the rest of my nectar-on-toast in a leaf and corking my thermos of thistledown tea, I studied the exotic biped.

His gray suit, chalky skin, mustache, and set jaw were indistinguishable from those of businessmen I'd seen pictured at the Learning Annex. There was only one difference: the color and pattern of his necktie.

I pushed off the toadstool and hovered above the grass, my wings beating the air. "I guess you won't be eligible for unemployment then." I couldn't resist showing off my knowledge of his world.

He nodded. "That's right." He yanked up handfuls of grass and sprinkled the dead green blades over the pants of his suit. He placed a cupped hand above his eyes and watched a flock of birds cross the blue sky.

"I don't mean to pry," I said, propelling myself to his eye level. "But what prompted you to leave during a board meeting? Did you disapprove of proposed budget changes?"

The businessman blinked. His eyes were the color of bluebells. "The walls started closing in on me."

Though I'd lived my entire life in the wood that surrounded the sun-dappled meadow in which I encountered the businessman, I was fairly certain that high-rise office buildings had stationary walls. "But how will you get by without a salary and an expense account and a key to the executive washroom?"

He shrugged. "I could always teach."

"What would you teach? Accounting? Systems Configuration? Interpersonal Workplace Politics?"

The businessman struggled out of his suit jacket, folded it, and placed it on the grass beside him. He unbuttoned the sleeves of his white shirt and rolled them above his elbows. He crossed his legs and gazed down at his shiny wingtips. "Dance," he said.

Flitting around his head, I nearly collided with his left ear. Nothing I'd seen at the Learning Annex had prepared me for this. "I didn't realize dance was part of the MBA curriculum."

"It's not," he said. "I do it on my own time."

I crossed my arms and hovered centimeters from his mustache. "Show me."

Rising, he stretched his arms above his head. He stood on his toes, reaching for the sky, then rolled his top half slowly down until his fingers brushed his wingtips and his nose was buried between his gray flannel calves. I had to admit that, for a businessman, he was flexible.

After kicking off his shoes and peeling off his thin black stockings, he set his feet wide and bent his right knee. He fell into a lunge, and a loud rip sounded. "I usually wear something looser when I dance," he said apologetically, stepping out of his torn pants. Below his yellow boxer shorts, his legs were thin and white, with red indentations where his stockings had cut off circulation. He loosened his tie, unbuttoned his white shirt, and stripped that off as well. He folded the shirt and stacked it neatly on top of his suit.

The businessman now stood in a white undershirt and boxer shorts, his hairy toes wriggling like spiders in the grass. His loosened tie hung limply around his neck. Unclothed, he no longer resembled the businessmen I'd seen at the Learning Annex, and it occurred to me that he could be some other kind of warm-blooded biped in disguise.

I returned to my toadstool and uncorked my thermos of thistledown tea. The businessman cleared his throat. "I don't think I can do this without music," he said.

"Pardon?"

"Music. Is there a way to get some music out here?"

I gazed across the meadow, my eyes passing over dragonflies, buttercups, dandelions, field mice, and grasshoppers to land on a cluster of crickets tuning up their wings. "What about crickets?" I said. "Could you shake it to the chirrup of crickets?"

He closed his eyes and dropped his head. The fingers of his left hand snapped five, six, seven, eight, and the businessman exploded out of his stance like a jubilant bomb.

I was spellbound. My forgotten thermos dangling from my fingers, I watched him spin and leap across the meadow. His feet seemed hardly to touch the ground; his white legs flashed with a fury I wasn't fast enough to follow. His back arched, his hips rolled, his necktie streamed behind him like a thin red and purple silk flag. Stretching his arms and neck, he turned and tumbled. His movements seemed dictated by the song of the crickets, who stridulated with a speed and intensity I'd never heard before. When he ended his dance with a knee slide across the meadow grass, salty droplets stood in the corners of my eyes.

Gasping for air, the businessman stood and walked in a circle with his hands on his hips. His dark hair glistened with sweat. Roses bloomed in his white cheeks. "Well," he said. "How was that?"

I am incapable of guile, and I knew if he looked into my golden eyes, the businessman would see right through me. So I turned away. Shrugged. "Not bad."

"Oh."

"Have you thought about your 401(k)?" I asked.

"What?"

"If you cash it out, you'll lose half of it in taxes."

He pulled on his white shirt. Started buttoning the buttons. "I'll probably roll it over into an IRA."

"Good," I said. "I guess you'd better start pounding the pavement tomorrow."

Stepping into his pants, he nodded. "Guess so."

Once his shirt was tucked in and his tie tightened, the businessman looked like himself again. Part of me was relieved; part of me was filled with regret.

"I guess I'm off then," he said.

"Will you be able to find your way back to your penthouse apartment?"

"I think so."

As he turned, I flitted up from my toadstool. "Wait!"

He stopped, and I propelled myself to his chest. "Take these," I said, offering my thermos and leaf-wrapped nectar-on-toast. "You must be starving." I placed the wrapped sandwich and thermos in his palm. They looked absurdly small, and we laughed, the businessman and I.

"So," he said.

"So." I touched down on his palm. Clasped my hands behind my back. As he lifted me to his gaze, I felt my face flush.

"My God," he said, "you're a beautiful little thing."

Bowing myself into a right angle, I kissed his cheek.

As he crossed the meadow and shrank from view, I saw the off-white walls of his corner office closing in on him and I wanted to scream. I wanted to fly after him and tell him his dance had melted my icy heart, that he'd made me want to give up leading woodsmen astray and sprinkling dust to devote myself to the study of warm-blooded bipeds full-time.

But I couldn't. In the world of warm-blooded bipeds, a businessman can count on a six-figure salary, an ample stock portfolio, and trips to the Caribbean twice a year. A teacher of dance can count on a meager paycheck and a lifetime of muscle aches and joint pains.

My stomach growling, I sat on the toadstool with my chin in my hands and my eye on the bottom line. The ghost of the businessman haunted the meadow grass, spinning and floating to the endless chirrup of the crickets, and I cursed myself for not gathering some proof of our encounter.

BURRO

Petra was twelve the day piñatas started talking. The inaugural incident occurred at a child's party in San Diego. Having been blindfolded and spun, the birthday boy was zigzagging over the lawn, slashing at the air with a broomstick, when the dangling, varicolored, tissue-papered burro his father had picked up at a twenty-four-hour Party Town opened its mouth and a string of syllables poured forth. These sounds engulfed the party, its guests and their astonished parents, the backyard of the split-level ranch, causing the boy's father, who was of Japanese extraction, to clap both hands to his face and exclaim, "Dios mío!"

But Spanish was not the language spoken by the piñata, nor by any of the piñatas that began vocalizing all over the world. The piñatas did not speak Portuguese, Italian, or French. Their language wasn't a Romance language at all, nor did it seem to be of Germanic, Slavic, Baltic, Altaic, Turkic, Mongolic, Semitic, or Sino-Tibetan origin. In fact, the language of the piñatas was related to no known tongue, and within a week, the world's supply of piñatas had been pulled from the shelves of party stores and *mercados* and transported to universities and laboratories, to be studied by linguists.

Among these linguists was Petra. Since she'd sat on the green shag in her parents' Texas den, viewing news reports about that first talking piñata, watching pandemonium descend on that San Diego backyard, Petra had known that she would dedicate her life to the mystery of the supernatural papier-mâché objects. And one spring morning when she entered her office—she was thirty-eight; eleven years had passed since she'd earned her doctorate, nine since she returned Michael's ring, explaining that though she loved him, there just wasn't room for a family, wasn't room in her life for anything but her work—Petra found that, as the voices of the piñatas arranged on wide metal shelves washed over her, she understood them. She sat at her desk, began transcribing their message.

An hour later, she put down her pen. She'd imagined, many times, what the piñatas might be saying. She'd imagined that their voices must be divine. That they longed to impart a directive, a key, a piece of wisdom that would make things clear, make them right. But as she read over her dictation, Petra found that the piñatas' concerns were entirely animal. They wanted to know why people had stopped filling them with candy. Why they'd stopped letting children beat them until they were torn asunder, until they could not be mended.

"We just assumed," Petra said, turning to the burros, "that you wanted us to stop."

Why? The orderly piñatas spoke with one bright voice.

"Because you can speak," she said. "Because you are important."

Then why, they said, *have you stuck us on these shelves?*

"To study you. To learn from you."

The piñatas exchanged glances. *Petra,* they said, *we were made to be filled, hung up, and destroyed. To let our bounty spill out and bring joy to children, and that is all we can do. There is nothing else we can teach you.*

"Seriously?" Petra shook her head. "Are you sure?"

As one, the burros nodded. *Positive.*

An hour later, Petra stood outside a twenty-four-hour Party Town, filling her trunk with bags of assorted candies. Once behind the wheel of her sedan, she hesitated, hand on key. In the store she'd spied a man who, for an instant, she'd imagined was Michael. She now wondered what his wife looked like, how many children they had, and what sort of candy the little devils might dive for when confronted with a ruptured piñata.

CHRYSALIS

Technically, it couldn't be classified as a coma. *Hypersomnolence,* a resident suggested. *Trance* or *spell* or *sopor,* said others. Not even the hospital's old guard spoke of the girl's condition with anything approaching certainty. The most she merited at rounds was a shrug of weary shoulders. *Hibernation? Hypnotism? Rapture?* Inevitably, one of the residents suggested a classic case of colossal torpidity, and everyone sniggered and moved on. Everyone but Dr. Bok.

He'd been on duty the day they found her prone on the waxed floor of the downtown library, *A Field Guide to Butterflies of North America* clutched in her right hand, index finger marking her place. His grandfather, an avid lepidopterist, had owned the same guide. *Vanessa atalanta,* about which the girl had been reading before she sank into her stupor, was quite striking, but the girl was no prize: dishwater blond, crooked mouth, wan, pitifully thin. Dr. Bok had intended to return *Field Guide* to the library when he left the hospital; instead, he carried the book to his cold two-room apartment and tucked it under his pillow. Each night, before removing his glasses and switching off the lamp, he perused the entry on *Vanessa atalanta.* In his dreams, the girl's pale eyelids fluttered like polychromatic wings in flight.

He spent his spare time studying catatonia. Stayed abreast of the latest developments. Sat beside Vanessa, as the nurses dubbed the girl, reading aloud from medical texts, mysteries, fairy tales. He shooed away orderlies, turning and bathing the girl himself. He arranged her hair and painted her nails. Dusted her pale cheeks with blusher. The other residents ribbed him mercilessly. When they dared him to wake her Prince Charming style, he rolled his eyes, but he thought about it. Kissing her cheeks and fingertips. Elbows and toes. Stomach. Thighs. Lips. He told her things he'd never told a soul. How his sister's stillbirth had destroyed his mother. How his grandfather, the lepidopterist, had been denatured by Alzheimer's.

When he entered Vanessa's room one spring morning to find the window wide open and the mattress littered with strands of blond hair and skin-hued fragments of casing, Dr. Bok wasn't really surprised. Before calling in the staff to ready the room for another patient, he sat beside the bed, studying the remnants of *Vanessa atalanta.* He wondered how long she'd perched on the cusp of her split pupa, damp from the chrysalis, drying her new body, waiting to take flight. She would never recognize him, nor would she recall anything he'd said or done—she was a brand-new being. This did not sadden him, however. Unlike most butterflies, *Vanessa atalanta* flies on sunny days even in winter, and Dr. Bok was certain that he would see her again. When he bumped into her on the street, whatever her outward aspect, he would know her. This conviction would sustain him for years to come.

Possible Wildlife in Road

All life is sacred. This I honestly believe. When I was six, my grandfather brought home Tillie, a calico cat rescued from a chemical testing facility. Tillie's fur was singed and patchy and her damaged eyes shone like small, iridescent oil slicks, but the abuse she'd suffered didn't soften her. She didn't think twice about upending insects, watching them struggle until they grew weak and then dead. She enjoyed letting mice dash for the safety of holes before stopping them with a paw on the threshold. When I witnessed Tillie tormenting smaller, weaker beings, I tried to save them, but it was always too late. I would gather what bits she did not devour and bury them in matchboxes, and I swore never to harm a living thing, to dedicate myself to the preservation of life. This is how, in spite of the way he was conceived, we ended up with Caleb.

Weekdays, I drop Caleb at school on my way to the animal hospital. Our home, a cabin accessible by a solitary dirt road, stands in a pine wood, and at times it seems the trees are encroaching, as though when I turn away and back, they've crept closer. We used to live in a bungalow in town, but we had to move on account of Tillie. Tillie isn't the cat I knew as a boy; she's my wife. Caleb's mother. The cat died years ago; my wife only sometimes wishes she were dead. She, too, bears the scars of what she's suffered, and when Tillie no longer felt safe in our bungalow, when she needed to put a great deal of distance between herself and other people, I was happy to oblige. I moved us to my great-grandfather's mountain cabin. We lived there for twelve years, and I thought we'd put the past behind us. Then I woke on a Wednesday to find Tillie's side of the bed empty. She'd left without so much as a note. When Caleb asked about his mother, I told him to get ready for school. I made a peanut butter and grape jelly sandwich and packed it in a paper sack with pretzels and a juice box. I hustled the boy out to my pickup, and we rode in silence through the pass.

Seventy-five years ago, WPA workers leveled a portion of a mountain known as Grandfather to build the highway, and on either side of this ravine, pines that are snowcapped from November to April cling to the sloping land. An abundance of creatures dwell in the surrounding wood—beavers and rabbits, wolves and foxes, black bears and whitetail deer—and I always navigate the pass on high alert, eyes roving, scanning the tree screen for any sign of a possum, groundhog, or wild turkey. Half the animals brought into the hospital have been struck down in the pass. I spend my days setting their bones, repairing perforated organs, stitching skin, but only a fraction of them pull through.

I was nine when my mother left us. A month later, I was riding through the pass with my grandfather, who used to let me sleep over at the cabin he'd helped his father build, when I saw a twelve-point buck step into the road. A man appeared to be dozing at the wheel of the F-150 beside us, and I struck my window, crying "Do something!" at my grandfather, who laid a hand on my thigh. He squeezed as he slowed the pickup, and for a suspended second, I thought machine and animal had canceled each other out—neither truck nor buck seemed to give ground—then the front of the F-150 crumpled and the deer was airborne. He came down in front of our truck, which crunched and thumped over him.

My grandfather had a knack for nursing injured animals back to health; his folk remedies and methods are more useful than much of what I learned in veterinary school. There was no hope for the buck, however, who ended up in bloody hunks on the shoulder, one antler torn clean off, his hind legs attached to the rest of him by a flap of hide. Afterward, my grandfather held me and stroked me in the cabin I would later share with Tillie and Caleb. A short time later, the DOT signs appeared in the pass.

"What does it mean?" Caleb asked at five, sitting on his knees, peering through the windshield, pointing at one of the signs. The boy had already taught himself to read; I was amazed and frequently intimidated by him.

"Lots of animals live in the woods," I said. "They tend to wander into the road, so you've got to keep your eyes peeled."

Caleb shook his blond head. "That's silly."

I agreed. "Watch for Animals" would have sufficed, or just plain "Deer Crossing." Whether something was or was not wildlife seemed to me straightforward, but the signs implied this was not the case; what wandered into the road looking like wildlife and walking like wildlife might not, in fact, be wildlife at all.

Seven years later, on the morning Tillie vanished, as I drove through the pass toward Caleb's school, I sneaked glances at the boy's face, which is an amalgam of my wife's and that of a stranger. He has Tillie's upturned nose and sharp chin, but his mouth is wider, his lips fuller. Tillie is dark; Caleb is blond and apple-cheeked like a cherub, and his eyes are a profound shade of green. Over the years I've tried to put together a picture of his father based on these features, because neither Tillie nor I ever saw the man's face. From my position on the floor, I couldn't—the angle was all wrong—and Tillie never opened her eyes. Once he growled a warning about not calling the cops and stole out through the bungalow's busted back door, once Tillie released me from the belts with which he'd hog-tied me, she climbed into the tub, where she spent some time scouring her skin with the precision of an automaton. Neither of us thought about the fact that she was destroying evidence.

The police never made an arrest, but two months later, just after we'd moved into the isolated cabin, just before Tillie told me she was pregnant, the detective who'd handled the investigation called to say they'd found a likely suspect burned to a crisp in a single-wide trailer. Daniel Mayo's record included assaults on women, and the night in question he'd been pulled over for a busted taillight two blocks from our bungalow. Tillie, who was no longer able to sleep through the night, who'd stopped teaching second grade and going to the grocery store, surprised me by refusing to let them take a DNA sample from then-unborn Caleb. "Don't you want to know?" I asked gently. "Won't it give you some peace?" Tillie shook her head. There was no more peace.

A photo of Mayo appeared in the paper, and I looked for traces of him in Caleb but found none. In the end I decided he couldn't have been the boy's father. I never would have said this aloud, but in my heart I knew Caleb's father was special. Extraordinary, even. For all his brutality, his sperm had triumphed where mine had always failed. Caleb emerged from Tillie's womb drenched in purity and beauty in spite of everything, and knowing his father is out there—at large—gives me some twisted and entirely inexplicable hope.

"Was it something I did?" Caleb asked, as we headed toward Millard Fillmore Middle School, breaking the silence that had bound us since we left the cabin. "Did she leave because of me?"

Something shook the branches of a roadside pine. I gripped the wheel with both hands and tapped the brakes, my eyes glued to the shuddering needles. "Of course not," I said. "Why would you ask that?"

Caleb shrugged. "Sometimes I think she wishes I'd never been born."

Tillie once told me she'd been dreaming of motherhood since she learned to crawl. She'd started stuffing pillows under her shirts at three, and in childhood games of make-believe she always took the role of mother. She'd spent her teen years babysitting, majored in early childhood education. When we met in the children's section of a bookstore, she'd been teaching second grade for three years. I told her I was looking for a book for a nonexistent nephew and she recommended some titles. Afterward, she let me buy her a latte in the bookstore café and we discovered that our grandfathers had served on the same destroyer in World War II. On our third date, I mentioned that I was eager to get married and start a family, and Tillie took me back to her apartment, where I stripped off her modest blouse and skirt and became acquainted with the dips and hollows of her angular, boy-like body. We started trying to conceive on our wedding night, and when I woke to discover Caleb's father looming over our bed, shrouded in shadow, pressing the blade of my own butcher's knife to my throat, ordering me to lie face-down on the floor, we'd been trying for four years.

"I can't," Tillie said from where she huddled in a corner of the cabin, wrapped in a green afghan crocheted by my great-grandmother. The pregnancy test lay where it had fallen on the heart pine floorboards after my wife hurled it against the wall.

Through its tiny plastic window, the pink lines for which we'd long been hoping were visible. "I can't have it."

"Tillie," I said, using the voice I employ with frightened animals—a voice picked up from my grandfather, who taught me how to move stealthily among the trees, to identify eggs in nests and fur clinging to bark and various paw- and hoofprints, who could quiet a badger, bear, or boy with a couple of carefully pitched words. I'd hardly dared touch my wife since the night Caleb was conceived, but I lowered myself to the floorboards and reached for her knee. She flinched. "A child isn't responsible for the sins of its father."

"I know."

"And we've been trying for so long."

"I know."

We'd often speculated about how quickly after conception a woman would feel the initial flicker of life, and I asked Tillie when she first suspected she was pregnant.

"When he was on top of me," she said after a pause. "Before he pulled out, I knew."

I felt stung by this revelation and wondered why she'd waited two months to take a pregnancy test, but I didn't ask. I lifted her chin with a finger, forcing her to look at me. Her dark eyes, once calm and even, now danced like windblown drops of rain. "You're the woman I love," I said, "and you *can* have this baby. I know you can."

"Doesn't it bother you?"

"What?"

"The thought of raising his child."

I shook my head. "The child deserves to live."

In the end, Tillie came around to my way of thinking. She carried the boy to term, and on a windy March morning I drove her through the pass, slowing to avoid a pair of possums and the fox that was shadowing them, coaching her on Lamaze breathing. All my people were long dead, but Tillie's parents and sister and nieces and nephew were there, and we captured every moment of the birth on video. I caught Caleb as he flowed from Tillie in a torrent of pink-tinged fluid. I clipped the umbilical cord and laid him on my wife's belly. I felt not the slightest twinge of regret, only joy and relief and an overpowering current of love, love that seemed to permeate the room, seeping into the corners. When I looked at Tillie, I thought she felt it, too. Despite the recurring nightmares I'd had before Caleb's birth—nightmares about Tillie batting him around and pinning him to the floor and tearing him to bits with the teeth and claws of a damaged and long-dead cat—she took to mothering like a raccoon takes to refuse. It seemed to calm her, to return her to the serene state she'd occupied before Caleb's father broke into our lives, which is why I was surprised to hear the boy say what he said about her wishing he'd never been born.

"That's ridiculous," I said, as we stopped in front of Millard Fillmore. "What's she ever done to give you that impression?"

Caleb hoisted his book bag onto his shoulder. His lips quivered. "It's just a feeling."

"Well, it certainly isn't true," I said. "Your mother loves you."

"I know she does."

"Very much."

"I know."

"Come here," I said, and Caleb slid across the bench seat until he was pressed against me. He'd recently turned twelve, but unlike most boys his age, he seemed to be growing more affectionate. Often he would still scramble into my lap. "He's getting too old, Walter," Tillie said into the darkness of our bedroom on more than one occasion. "It isn't right." "Would you rather he was shaving his head and spitting at us?" "Of course not. You know what I mean."

And though I feigned ignorance, I *did* know. Caleb's delicate nature would bring him nothing but sorrow, but I couldn't bring myself to discourage it. As I watched him stroke the exposed belly of a terrier at the hospital or felt his arms snake around my waist from behind, my feelings for the boy swelled painfully, squeezing my lungs until I was forced to gasp for air. "It can be a lot scarier than you'd think," my grandfather used to say, after my mother left us. "Loving your own damn child." He would imprison me on his bony lap, gulping Old Grand-Dad and weeping, and I was appropriately terrified by the thought of such desperate love.

"I'll bet Mom went to see Aunt Carly," Caleb said now, as I buried my nose in his curls, which smelled of sun-dried cotton. Tillie's sister had moved to the Piedmont with her family two years earlier. The boy's explanation for his mother's absence reminded me of scenarios I'd come up with after my own mother's departure, and although I knew he was wrong, I told him I was sure he was right. I tickled him until he squealed, then watched him trundle inside. The sky hovered over the school like the iron hull of the destroyer Tillie's and my grandfathers served on in World War II, and as I drove to the animal hospital, snow started drifting.

It was the war that convinced my grandfather of the sanctity of life. To escape detection by the Japanese, he'd once buried himself under a pile of his slain comrades, and for the rest of his days he would wake periodically, shrieking, trying to shove his buddies off him, screaming about their blood, how it burned his skin. Whenever this happened, I held him until he quieted, but my mother just rolled her eyes. "He's no saint, you know," she would say, dragging on a filterless cigarette. On the day she left for parts unknown, I found a sealed envelope under my pillow, one on which she'd written *If you're ready for the truth, open me.* I buried the envelope in my sock drawer, where it waited for years, yellowing patiently.

"I've got something to tell you," Tillie said into the inky darkness of our bedroom the night before she disappeared. This was when we discussed vital things—after we'd switched off the bronco-shaped bedside lamps my grandfather bought at auction while I was in my mother's womb. "Something I've kept from you for twelve years."

My mouth went dry, and I swallowed.

"It's about Caleb's father," she said. "I lied when I said I never saw his face."

I felt angry, but not because she'd lied. This was a jealous anger, one I tried to quell as I reached for her hand under the bedclothes. "Tillie, what are you saying?"

Darkness spread itself through the rooms of the cabin so densely that our pupils were never able to adjust, and in the still of night we were forced to make our way to the bathroom like the blind, our outstretched fingers acting as eyes. I couldn't see Tillie, but I felt her turning toward me. "When he tied you up," she said, "when he yanked up my nightgown, I was terrified, but I never felt any pain, so I peeked, and when I did my fear vanished. Caleb's father was seven feet tall, and he was crowned by soft light. He wore a cape and boots, and his body was covered in downy fur. He had horns, Walt, huge white horns that wound around and around. His teeth looked so sharp, but he was smiling the whole time. And crying. His eyes were the color of ancient moss. I heard a deep, melodious voice, and I realized he was speaking to me with his eyes. He kept saying this wasn't an act of violence. *I am a creature of love,* he said. *I venture out of the wood only to deliver love wherever it is needed.*"

Tillie paused for breath, and I was glad she couldn't see my face. I wondered how I could have been so blind to her unraveling.

"He said he was giving me what I wanted most, that Caleb would be extraordinary because he was conceived of pure love. Once he'd gone, I doubted what I'd seen and heard, and yet, there was Caleb. I thought he might come out with horns and a halo. I've been struggling with this for twelve years, going back and forth, but the memory hasn't faded, and I'm convinced now that everything happened just as I remember it." Tillie squeezed my hand, which had gone numb. "Say something, Walt."

What could I say? That I, too, believed Caleb's father was special, but that I drew the line at the notion of a mythical man-beast roaming the earth, impregnating women in the name of love? That I'd been in the room when Caleb was conceived, and that, to me, what happened between Tillie and Caleb's father had sounded like an act of violence? That when the man wasn't grunting and moaning, I'd heard him saying lewd and disparaging things? That when my wife wasn't sobbing, I'd heard her begging him to get off? To leave her alone? That lying on the floor of our bungalow with my hands and feet bound behind me, I'd felt more powerless than I used to feel when my grandfather pulled off his pajama bottoms and pressed himself against me in the night? That knowing even the most unthinkable act could result in a being as pure as Caleb was the only thing that had prevented me from going against my own deeply held belief and taking my life?

"Why are you telling me this now?" I said.

"It's time Caleb knew the truth."

"The truth?"

"About his father."

"You're going to tell him what you just told me."

"Yes."

"I don't know," I said. "He's still pretty young."

"He's almost a teenager." She squeezed my hand. "We both know how special Caleb is. Don't you think it's time he knew, too?"

Once Tillie was sleeping, I stole down the blackened hall, feeling my way. I pushed open the door of Caleb's room, and there, in the glow of an owl-shaped night-light my grandfather bought me when I was a boy, I knelt beside Caleb's bed. I pushed the curls from his damp forehead, and he sighed and turned toward me. As far as the boy knew, I was his father. Tillie and I had never before discussed telling him the truth about his parentage. I saw no point in shattering his illusions, but he was her son, and I'd always deferred to her when it came to Caleb. I knew the boy would be confused by his mother's version of events, that he would come to me with questions. I considered scooping him up and stealing out to my pickup. Driving through the pass, just the two of us, heading for parts unknown. He would never realize I wasn't his father. He would never understand how his conception had damaged his mother. As I pictured us rolling over sun-drenched blacktop, I stroked his sleeping limbs. I thought of my grandfather, and fear fluttered within me. In the dimness of the owl's light, Caleb looked unnaturally beautiful—godly—and I wished his eyes would open, that he would throw his arms around my neck.

The next morning I surreptitiously examined the boy as he ate Fruity Pebbles and drank orange juice. I'd never before noticed that the green of his eyes was so like the color of moss. After dropping him at school, I drove through increasingly heavy snow to the hospital, where I was instantly wrapped in the comfort of contained chaos. I examined a steady stream of Labradors and poodles, spaniels and collies, mutts and housecats, parakeets and rabbits. To my dismay, I was forced to put down an Irish setter who'd got hold of a poisoned steak. Rex's distended tongue lolled from his mouth, and his eyes spun, unfocused. His limbs jerked, his breath was ragged, but worst of all was his plaintive keen. Rex's owner stood beside the exam table, stroking the ginger dog, cursing his neighbor, who he was sure had put out the poisoned meat. "Rex tore up one of his flowerbeds last year," the old man said, shaking his head. "The bastard's never forgiven him." After administering sodium pentobarbital, I retired to my office, where I sat weeping until the receptionist buzzed to tell me a black bear cub had been struck down in the pass.

The teen boys who brought in the cub smelled of whiskey, and I decided the mother bear must have been dead already not to have torn them apart as soon as they stepped from their truck. The cub was unconscious. His hind legs were broken and blood leaked from lacerations on his abdomen and chest. I went to work with another vet and two nurses, cleaning, suturing, setting bones. Once the plaster casts were in place, we moved him into an oxygenated recovery tent. Only time would tell if the cub would live.

After removing a tumor from the back of a guinea pig and extracting a three-foot length of dental floss from the intestine of a kitten, I changed out of my scrubs and headed home. Darkness had fallen, but light shed by the waxing gibbous moon bounced off a blanket of snow, infusing the air with a ghostly brightness. In the pass, I drove ten miles under the limit, searching for wildlife. Snowflakes swirled in white tunnels thrown out by my headlamps, and I'd almost reached the turnoff to the cabin when I spied a hunched figure moving along the shoulder—a man, remarkably tall, wrapped in a hooded cloak. I wondered what in the hell he thought he was up to. Even an experienced woodsman like my grandfather wouldn't have ventured out on such a night.

After passing the man, I looked for him in my rearview. Had he ducked into the trees? I eased the truck onto the shoulder, turned and surveyed the white road, but saw no movement. As the heater hummed, I considered pulling the flashlight out of the glove box, stepping out to investigate. Perhaps he was in need of help. I pictured myself wandering down the road, peering into the trees, calling myself hoarse. But for drifting snow, the pass was still. Minutes ticked by and I became less and less certain that I'd seen a man at all. A sense of desolation crept through me. My gloved fingers trembled as I put the truck in gear.

At home, I told Caleb that Tillie had called the hospital, that she was visiting her sister as he'd suggested. When he asked why she'd gone without telling us, I said she needed some alone time. When he asked if we were getting a divorce, I assured him that we were not. Caleb nodded, but I don't think he believed me. That night, we ate spaghetti and watched *The Night of the Hunter*, a movie I used to watch with my grandfather, who couldn't abide death scenes. He refused to watch war movies but he loved sleepy-eyed Robert Mitchum. He passed this affection on to me, and I to Caleb. As we huddled on the couch under the same afghan Tillie had been wrapped in when she discovered she was pregnant, I studied Harry Powell's shadow. On the night Caleb was conceived, his father had thrown a similar shade on the wall of our bedroom—long, with a large, misshapen head. From where I lay bound on the floor, I'd studied this shadow carefully, trying to block out the sounds, humming the old-time hymns I used to hum when my grandfather slid his hands into my underpants. On the couch, Caleb now pushed against me, and I wound my arms around him.

Two days later, after dropping Caleb at school, I sailed right past the hospital. I followed Main Street to Madison and turned from there onto Jefferson, slowing as I approached the brick bungalow where Tillie and I had lived at the outset of our marriage. The house in which Caleb was conceived. Not wanting to taint the place for its new owners, we hadn't told the young couple what happened there. "What if he comes back?" Tillie had said. "Shouldn't we warn them?" I assured her that perpetrators only return to the scene of the crime in movies. As I cruised by, I realized that, though the shutters and door had a fresh coat of paint, the house was devoid of life. A red and white *For Sale* sign was staked next to the front walk.

Wondering what had become of Ricky and Sue Scott, I drove to the hospital, where I found the bear cub awake. He was weak, but he would live. Burying my face in his fur, I nuzzled his sutured stomach, and he wrapped his front paws around my head in what seemed an embrace. I attributed his recovery to age. Young bodies are miraculously resilient. *Children abide.* In time, they can recover from abuse that would permanently damage or kill an adult.

After tucking Caleb in that night, I tossed and turned. I rolled my truck down the hill before starting the engine. There was no sign of the tall, cloaked figure in the pass. I headed into town, toward Jefferson Street. For several years after we'd moved, I suffered from terrible insomnia—at times, I still do—and when I couldn't sleep, I would sneak out of the cabin and drive through the pass. I would park outside the brick bungalow on Jefferson, where I was sure Ricky and Sue Scott were sleeping peacefully or making love, and I would imagine Caleb's father returning. I would consider how the sight of him might affect my belief in the sanctity of life. On several occasions, after watching for some time, I exited my pickup and moved stealthily around the house, checking every door and window.

Ricky and Sue Scott left the back door open once, and I walked right in. I examined the kitchen in the dim light of the bulb over the sink. Someone had left a butcher's knife on the counter, and I studied its softly glowing blade. The Scotts hadn't gotten around to replacing the avocado-colored 1970s appliances, and I was overcome by an uncanny sensation of trespassing in my own home. I crept all over, rifling through cabinets and closets, sitting on unfamiliar chairs and couches. I wondered, as I went, if Caleb's father had stopped to paw through our belongings or if he'd made a beeline for the bedroom. The sound of Ricky's and Sue's deep, even breathing flowed through the house, filling every crevice, and as I slunk toward their king-size bed, I thought about how long Caleb's father might have stood, listening to the sound of Tillie's and my breathing. Had he been nervous, or was this something he'd done a dozen times before? I tried to picture myself pressing the blade of the knife I'd seen in the kitchen to Ricky's throat. Sue was a lovely blond, and I tried to imagine shoving up her nightgown, yanking down her panties despite her protestations, despite the tears that would no doubt flow. As if my thoughts had penetrated her rest, Sue stirred. Sitting up, she looked right at me. A streetlamp partially illuminated the room, and I waited for her scream to pierce the quiet of Jefferson Street, but Sue didn't scream. She sighed—a deep, satisfied sound—before rolling over and pressing herself into her husband from behind.

Jefferson was dark, but as I rolled to a stop in front of the bungalow, I noticed a light burning. I found the back door open. Inside, the rooms were bare and empty. Even the kitchen had been stripped. I moved silently through the dim, familiar space toward what had once been our bedroom and found Tillie curled on the floor, her blue wool coat thrown over her. I shook her shoulder. She sat up expectantly, but when she saw me her smile fled.

"Oh," she said. "It's you."

I lowered myself to the hardwood. "Not who you were expecting."

"I'm waiting for Caleb's father."

"They only return to the scene of the crime in movies, remember?"

Tillie took my hands. She'd been gone three days. She looked exhausted, disheveled. The weight of my fear for her overwhelmed me, and my eyes stung.

"You don't believe me," she said, "and Caleb won't either."

"What did you plan to do?"

"Ask him to show himself to his son." Tillie smiled, and I was confronted with the second-grade teacher I'd met in a bookstore fifteen years earlier. "If you'd seen him, you would understand. Oh, Walt. I wish you hadn't been tied up that night."

Over the years, I'd given a lot of thought to what might have happened if I hadn't been tied up the night Caleb was conceived. If I'd heard his father breaking in and had merely been feigning sleep as he stole into the room. If I'd leapt from our bed and concealed myself behind the door to lie in wait. If I'd had the foresight to stash a weapon in my bedside table. If I'd been able to loose myself, to rise from the floor while Caleb's father was still on top of my wife. Would I have been able to sneak up behind him, to sink a knife between his shoulder blades?

"I *do* believe you, Tillie," I said, and though I didn't, I wanted to and hoped that in time I would. I wanted to believe the man-beast existed. It wouldn't be the first time I'd rejected the truth in favor of something more palatable. When I was sixteen, my grandfather threw a blood clot and I was forced to drive his old F-150 through the snowy pass, trying in vain to reach the hospital before the clot reached his heart. Afterward, I returned to the cabin, removed the unopened letter that had been languishing in my sock drawer for seven years, and burned it.

Before my grandfather stopped breathing, as he'd leaned his trembling head on my shoulder, as his gnarled fingers clutched at my lap, he tried to confess things he'd done to my mother. He tried to beg forgiveness for things he'd done to me. He tried to make excuses, but I wouldn't let him. Over the reedy sound of his voice, I hummed the old-time hymns. Once he was gone, I would be alone in the world, and no matter what he'd done, I didn't want him to die. I wanted him to live forever. He'd taught me everything I knew, and I believed I loved him with all my heart. When he stopped breathing, I pounded the steering wheel and howled. In front of the hospital, I lowered his lids and called him "Grandfather Mountain," the nickname I'd given him as a boy. Two months later, I lied about my age and enlisted in the navy. Four years after that, I put myself through veterinary school working as a CPR instructor and lifeguard.

Having promised to help Tillie explain to Caleb his conception, I convinced her to leave the bungalow. Her car was parked on a side street, but we left it and climbed into my pickup. Tillie slid over until she was pressed against me. She laid her head on my shoulder. As we drove, snow started falling, and by the time we hit the pass, it was coming down in fat flakes. Tillie breathed evenly into my ear, and I thought of how, in the months leading up to Caleb's birth, I'd considered leaving her. It had nothing to do with Tillie or the way Caleb was conceived; I'd convinced her to have him, and I believed in his right to live. I wanted a child, but I feared that my grandfather had tainted me with his love—a love that choked the man, a love that kicked him in the gut every damned day of his life. But once Caleb was born, I learned to appreciate the torment of such unspeakable love. I also learned that urges and actions are entirely separate things.

As we approached the turnoff, I imagined the sleeping boy, and my heart swelled. I gasped for air, and that was when I saw it—a tall, cloaked figure darting from the white-coated pines, bounding in front of my pickup to cross the road. It turned toward my headlights, and I thought I saw curled white horns and moss-green eyes that dragged the depths of me, but before I could wake my wife or say "Tillie" it was gone, scurrying into the snowy wood. Momentarily, I understood that life is just death yanked inside out. Then the moment ended, and it was me in my pickup with Tillie's head on my shoulder, shivering with the remnants of awareness, guiding us carefully through the pass.

Breach

When she saw it in the electronics aisle at the Goodwill on Cheviot, the one that gets all the best tracksuits, Vera's first thought was *Now why would anyone in their right mind want to buy that?* She was more capable than most of seeing the value in the cast-off goods of others, but Vera couldn't for the life of her figure out why any sane human being would purchase a single walkie-talkie. And she was about to say so when Maureen reached out and plucked the transceiver from its dusty plywood shelf.

"Say," said Maureen. "Nice, huh?"

Vera could recall buying walkie-talkies for her children years earlier, and she was sure they'd been black with a red button, just like the one Maureen was, unbelievably, placing in her cart, where it now rested against an oval gold leaf mirror and five taped-together painted-daisy juice glasses and three pairs of Lee Rider jeans, the discontinued kind with the high waist and the flat front, the jeans Maureen was forever searching for.

"Ready?" Maureen said.

Silent in her consternation, Vera trailed after Maureen, who pushed her cart toward the counter, rocking her hips to the faint strains of "Dancing on the Ceiling." They'd been in their twenties when the song came out, both married, both with babies. Over the years, they'd seen each other through three divorces and two dead children. Eating disorders. Sexually transmitted diseases. Cancer scares. A hysterectomy. They voted the same way, enjoyed the same romantic movies, clipped the same coupons. Whenever she came across a matched set of anything—cowboy boots, horse-head bookends, rhinestone earrings, elbow-length gloves—Vera saw herself and Maureen. She couldn't help it. One just didn't make sense without the other.

Dinah, who was ringing up Maureen, held the solitary walkie-talkie aloft. "Where's the other one?" she said.

Maureen turned to Vera. She winked. "That's what I'd like to know."

On the way home, Vera studied Maureen, who sat behind the wheel smiling, humming a tune Vera couldn't place. Vera looked down, into a dark chasm that had opened between the driver and passenger seats of the Pontiac. She saw Maureen sitting at her gold-flecked Formica table, depressing the red button, speaking softly, telling whomever might be listening things she would never tell Vera.

Mysteries that were Maureen's alone.

Victoria

"This," said Sid, holding Queen Victoria aloft, "is not your best work."

Darryl nodded. Sid wasn't telling him anything he didn't know. A blind man could have seen it. A blind mole rat could have seen it.

"Dare I ask," Sid continued, "where this creepy sonofabitch came from?"

The fur that, in a more just world, might have covered Victoria's nudity seemed to have sprouted up on Darryl's tongue, and the furniture in his wood-paneled living room was looking distinctly diagonal. It felt as though his head had been flattened and stretched, like an acoustic membrane over an in-use kick drum, and he wore nothing but a stained bathrobe and a pair of secondhand sandals in the style of those worn by Jesus Christ, their footbeds blackened by the bare soles of a stranger.

"I've got the feeling," said Darryl, attempting once, twice, and failing to push up from where he lay, his right temple on one of those braided rag rugs Alma got from the Latinas at the flea market, saliva tethering his mouth to the floorboards, "that I've had a visitation."

"A visitation?" Sid watched his brother struggle to gain verticality. He made no move to help. "From who?"

"From *whom*." After propelling himself to his knees, then to his feet, Darryl stood swaying, trying to gather the power to step toward Sid, who was now balancing the contorted, hairless form of Queen Victoria on his outstretched palm. "The object pronoun is *whom,* Sid. You know that."

"Jesus." Sid shook his head. "I think you're channeling Dad."

"Yes." Darryl picked up one foot, put it down in front of the other. Heel/toe. Heel/toe. Nice and steady. This is walking. Once he got going, it wasn't nearly so improbable as it had seemed from the floor. "Yes, my visitation was from Dad."

"Dad?"

"Yes."

"The Dad who disappeared ten years ago?"

"That's the one."

"Did he bring you the mole rat?"

Darryl bypassed his brother, rounded the dining table, wobbled toward the door through which he would find the kitchen, in which he would find the liquor cabinet, in which he would find the whiskey. "Sid," Darryl said without turning back, certain that any movement of his eyes would blow him off course, that if he looked away for even an instant he would end up straying into the bathroom perhaps, or the bedroom he'd shared with Alma for nine years, or the big hall closet, or his studio, in which he stretched the tanned hides of animals, both wild and domestic, depending on the job, over polyurethane foam he'd shaved and molded into the shape of a charging black bear, or a twelve-point buck paused in a clearing, gazing majestically into the beyond, or a tabby cat arching its back on a windowsill, or a poodle dancing on its hind legs—the room in which, five days earlier, Darryl had beaten the shit out of Spencer, Alma's fourteen-year-old son. "Can I get you a drink?"

"Darryl," Sid said, following his brother into the kitchen, "where are Alma and Spence?"

"Gone." Darryl opened an overhead cabinet, plucked out

a bottle half full of Jack Daniel's. He rinsed two glasses at the sink, turned toward the Formica table centrally positioned on the blue-tiled floor. Sid had seated himself in an upholstered chair, one of a set Alma acquired at the flea market for a song, after exercising her own undeniably brutal brand of bargaining, and he'd placed Queen Victoria at the table's center. Darryl sat, opened the bottle, filled the glasses liberally. "Are you aware," he said, sliding one of these toward his brother, "that the naked mole rat is indigenous to the horn of Africa?"

"I'm not." Sid eyed his glass. "That's a serious drink."

Darryl lifted his own glass, drained it, poured another. The alcohol's toxins went to work on his nervous system and he felt a welcome lifting, a lessening of pain. His eyes stung with grateful tears, which he blinked out of existence. "I didn't know you were in town, Sid."

"I wasn't," said Sid. "I've only just arrived."

"To what do we owe the pleasure?"

Sid sipped his whiskey. "Mom called. She's worried about you."

"They live in colonies," Darryl said, shaking his head to clear it. "Like bees. Or ants. You know that? In systems of underground burrows. Beneath the desert sands. There's a queen, even, and drones. Only the queen can reproduce, and her offspring are raised communally. The other females' fertility is suppressed."

"Are we talking about mole rats?"

Darryl nodded.

Sid plucked Queen Victoria from the tabletop. "Jesus," he said, turning her over in his hands. "He must have been a real pain in the ass to work with. I mean, he's not very goddamned big, is he?"

"*She,*" said Darryl. "You're holding the queen of the naked mole rats."

As Sid studied Victoria, Darryl studied his brother, who looked more like their father each time Darryl saw him, which wasn't often. Unlike Darryl, Sid had fled from home as soon as he was able, had gone to college in Maryland and then moved to New York, where he'd been working in advertising and trying to "make it" as a playwright for twenty-five years. A couple of Sid's plays had been produced off-off-Broadway, but they'd never garnered favorable reviews, and Sid was now closing in on fifty. He'd acquired their father's paunch and his hair was silvering in the same way. He even wore glasses identical to the black-framed spectacles Darryl Chase Sr. had worn.

When Darryl looked at Sid, he saw their father in the ramshackle outbuilding behind the house they grew up in, bowed over the hide of a deer or a German shepherd, carefully scraping it clean, removing all traces of fat and flesh with a knife, or shaping, with a pair of pliers, braided lengths of wire into the outline of an animal's haunch or snout. A high school English teacher by trade, Darryl Chase Sr. honestly felt that he'd been called by God to the divine art of taxidermy. It was the only thing that gave him peace, that quelled the rage bubbling just beneath his surface, threatening to spew, to coat the world in a deadly pall of vitriol, of molten matter and ash. Nothing could be more maddening, Darryl Sr. had often declared, than trying to teach teenagers how to properly wield their own goddamned native tongue. Left alone with his creatures, he might have been a wholly different man. "The beauty of it," he said once to his eldest son, as they lay twined together on the mattress Darryl Sr. had installed in a corner of his taxidermy studio, "is that I get to build them from the ground up. They resemble what they were in life, but once I mount them, they become something else. Better than their best selves. I find their ultimate attitude and I freeze them into it eternally. It looks like life, but it's better. Clean. Quiet. With none of life's pain. None of its doubts."

I know what you did.

"What?" Darryl hadn't seen his brother's lips move. "What was that?"

Sid deposited Queen Victoria back in the center of the table. He shook his head. "I didn't say anything."

"You did."

"I didn't."

The brothers Chase blinked at one another.

"You sure?"

Sid lifted a hand and crossed two fingers over his heart, just as they'd done when they were kids.

Darryl poured himself a drink. "You know who taught me about the naked mole rat?" he said.

Sid shook his head.

"Spencer," said Darryl. "God, he's a smart kid. The kind I would have kicked the shit out of in grade school. The kind of kid who might actually have given Dad some small hope. Spence does well in all his subjects. He's like a walking encyclopedia, if you want to know the truth. And it must come from his real father, 'cause he certainly doesn't get it from Alma. She loves Spencer and all—I mean, she *is* his mother—but ever since Spence learned to talk, she hasn't been able to stand him. The boy does tend to go on and on, about any number of subjects. It gets annoying, sure, but it drives Alma up the wall. Spence regularly sends her into a blind rage. She hits him. Really whales on the kid. Sometimes I have to intervene."

You can't hide what you did.

"What was that?"

Sid shook his head. "I didn't say anything."

Darryl looked at Queen Victoria. He turned the mole rat to face him. She was without a doubt the ugliest animal he'd ever mounted.

"So a couple of weeks ago," Darryl continued, "Spence was getting obsessed with these naked mole rats. Just obsessed. And I decided to take him to the zoo in Atlanta, where they've got a colony. Alma thought if she was trapped in the cab of the pickup with Spence for three solid hours, and he was talking about the mole rats, she'd strangle him, so she elected not to come. They had the mole rats in the House Rodentia, along with marmots, prairie dogs, chinchillas, porcupines, voles, that type of thing, and they had it set up so you could look through this Plexiglas window and see them in their burrows, writhing together, a mob of pink, wrinkled, nearly hairless bodies, a mass of scrabbling claws and giant dirty-yellow buckteeth."

"Ugh," said Sid. "Sounds horrifying."

"It was," said Darryl, "but Spencer absolutely fucking loved it. The kid stood there for two solid hours, staring. I kept going off, buying popcorn and sodas, checking out the other animals. I finally pulled Spence away, got him over to the primate house. We went and saw the new tiger. And the baby giraffe. But Spencer kept begging me to take him back to the House Rodentia. So I did. And as we stood there, staring through the window into that crush of naked mole rats, Spence started telling me about these things. He'd named them, see, and made up stories about their lives, about their relationships. It was nuts, the level of detail this kid imagined. Their queen was named Victoria, and she ruled the other mole rats with an iron fist. Or paw or whatever. Absolutely iron. There were two mole rats in there named Justin, and one named Bernard. There was a really little one called Tina. And as we watched, I started getting angry.

I started thinking that someone needed to do something about that fucking queen and her tyranny. That someone needed to bring Victoria's reign to an end."

You'll never bury it deep enough. No matter how hard you try.

Darryl picked up Queen Victoria, brought the mole rat close to his face. He'd mounted her with mouth wide open, her four incisors exposed. Darryl poked the tip of a pinky inside her mouth. He looked up at his brother. Sid's manicured fingers appeared to be choking his glass, which was still half full.

"Are you telling me," said Darryl, "that you didn't hear that?"

"Hear what?"

Darryl indicated Sid's glass. "Drink up," he said, "baby brother."

Sid swallowed the remaining whiskey, pushed his glass slowly toward Darryl. As Darryl poured, Sid stood. He crossed to the counter, braced himself against it. "Before," he said, "when you asked why I was here, I wasn't entirely honest. The truth is, I'm not just here because Mom's worried about you. There's something else. Something I have to tell you."

Darryl thought about standing, thought that for some reason he should, but he knew that he would never make it. His legs felt tremulous, like rubber bands or overcooked manicotti. "I thought we were talking," he said, "about naked mole rats."

Sid nodded. "Go on."

"That night in the motel room," said Darryl, "I couldn't sleep. I sat up beside Spence's bed, watching him. He's a beautiful kid, really. I mean, objectively speaking, he's just lovely. And lots of times, when I can't sleep at home, I do the same thing. Sit up and watch him. Sometimes I touch him, lightly, on top of his head, or on one of his cheeks. But that night in the motel, I couldn't stop thinking about Victoria. I'd brought a fifth of

Wild Turkey and I was drinking straight from the bottle, and I left Spence alone in the room. I drove back to the zoo. I climbed the fence, used a crowbar to break into the House Rodentia, which was not terribly well secured. I got into the room where zookeepers had recreated the arid desert habitat of eastern Africa. I dropped to my hands and knees beside this big sand pit and I dug until I hit the colony's system of interconnected burrows. The mole rats were terrified, squealing. They kept biting me, trying to protect their queen. But Victoria was twice as big as the others, and I finally found her, way down at the bottom. I yanked her free, and then I ran like hell."

"Jesus," said Sid. "Are you shitting me?"

Darryl shook his head. He crossed his heart with two fingers.

"Jesus," Sid said again.

"Queen Victoria kept biting me viciously, so I had her in a kind of stranglehold, and it wasn't until I got back to the motel that I realized I'd killed her. Or maybe she died of fright. I didn't know. I just knew she was dead. And I knew from what Spence had told me that, at that moment, back in the House Rodentia, the rest of the female naked mole rats were battling to determine who would take her place. So I folded Victoria's limp, wrinkled body in a hand towel from the motel and tucked her into the glove box.

"When we got back from Atlanta, I worked on mounting her for days. It was tricky. As you can see, she's pretty fucking small, and her skin's so thin. It was like trying to tan a Kleenex. But finally I got her mounted. I thought Spence would be thrilled. But when he opened the box I'd wrapped her in, when he lifted her out, he started crying. I mean really bawling. *How could you!* he screamed. *Murderer! You murdered their queen!* I tried to explain that I'd preserved Victoria, that I'd made her even better than she was in life, but Spence didn't believe me. He just kept calling me a monster. He was thrashing and kicking at me. At some point, I guess I hauled off and hit him in the face. It felt good, so I did it again. And again."

That afternoon, Alma packed a couple of bags and she and Spence departed for the Christmas tree farm where her sister lived with her family, fifty miles from Darryl's split-level ranch. When Darryl pointed out to Alma that she hit Spence with some regularity, she said, "Spence is mine to do with as I will. The two of us are bound by blood, and blood grants you certain rights. Permission. Absolution."

"Think they'll be back?" said Sid, from where he stood against the kitchen counter.

Darryl nodded. "We've been a family a long time."

"Good," said Sid. "I'm glad to hear it."

Someone's going to dig it up. Someone's going to find out what you've done.

This time, Darryl didn't bother to look at his brother. He picked up Queen Victoria and cradled her to his chest.

"Darryl," said Sid, "I've written a memoir. And the thing is, the book's going to be published. And you have the right to know that, in it, I talk about Dad."

"Dad?"

Sid nodded. "I'm sure this won't be easy for you to hear, but in the book I talk pretty frankly about what he did to you."

"To me? What did Dad do to me?"

"Darryl."

"Do you know," said Darryl, finding the strength to stand at last, pushing up to his feet, stepping over the tiles toward his brother, still clutching the queen of the naked mole rats to his chest, "what I found inside Victoria? What I discovered when I sliced open her belly?"

Sid moistened his lips with the tip of his tongue, the way Darryl Chase Sr. always had. He shook his head.

"Babies," said Darryl, pressing his face close to Sid's. "A litter of pups. Seven in all. Nearly fully formed. Seven tiny, tightly curled mole rats. And do you know what I did with them?"

Sid shook his head again.

"I buried them," said Darryl. "I tucked each of those unborn babies into an empty matchbox and I buried them in the backyard. Under the black walnut. Right next to Dad. I buried those naked mole rats all around Dad."

* * *

According to Lila Sparrow, the realtor who sold her the property, the bodies of Darryl Chase Sr. and his younger son, Sidney, had long ago been exhumed from the backyard, but still Francine couldn't stop digging. Ostensibly she was preparing the yard for a landscaping overhaul. In the southwest corner would be a vegetable garden and in the southeast a plot for the cultivation of exotic plant species. In the northeast corner, under the shade of the black walnut, Francine would install a rock garden with iron benches and a rustic shelter. When New York acquaintances asked what had prompted her sudden move to North Carolina, when they asked if she'd purchased the split-level ranch in the middle of nowhere solely because of its macabre history, Francine denied the allegation, but Francine was a liar. In fact, the house's story had everything to do with her decision to uproot her family, to move her elderly father and her fourteen-year-old daughter to a part of the nation none of them had ever seen.

"Mom. Mom!"

Francine looked up into the face of her child. "Yes?"

"What are you doing out here?" Eva dropped a hand on Francine's shoulder, gave her mother a well-rehearsed look of concern. "Shouldn't you be in the house? You know, like, getting to work on your book already?"

Francine prayed for summer's end. She wanted the demands of a new year at a new school to occupy her daughter's time and energy. She was about to tell Eva to buzz off, and then she caught sight of Malcolm sitting in the southeast corner of the yard. "What the hell's Dad doing?" she said.

Eva tented a hand over her eyes, swiveled toward her grandfather. "Painting," she said. "I helped him put together the easel this morning. Dr. Russo recommended it. He says the making of art can be very therapeutic."

"What's he painting?"

Eva swiveled back toward her mother. She grinned. "You, of course."

Francine pushed up from where she knelt in the shade of the black walnut. She adjusted her wide-brimmed gardening hat, sipped from her water bottle.

"Goddamn it!" roared her father. "Quit moving around! Why can't you hold still?"

"What are you wearing?" said Francine, looking at Eva.

Eva shrugged. "A bathing suit."

"We don't have a pool."

"I was going to sunbathe."

"Don't you think," said Francine, "that your time would be better spent practicing the viola? Or writing thank you notes for that mountain of birthday presents under which your bedroom is currently buried?"

Eva shook her head. She skipped ten feet away from her mother, checked the position and angle of the sun, unfurled, with a snap, the towel tucked beneath one slender arm, then stretched out facedown upon it. Francine watched her daughter point her toes, watched Eva's bottom, barely covered by an orange bikini, switch back and forth ever so slightly.

"If you're not wearing sunscreen," Francine said, pulling her hat into place and dropping back to her knees, "I don't want to know."

"Francine!" roared Malcolm. "Come on!"

She plunged her spade again and again into the dark, loamy earth, allowed its welcoming metallic scent to wash over her. As a child, Francine had eaten dirt, a habit her father, whose wife died giving birth to Francine, never forced his daughter to break. Increasing age and the disapproval of her peers had eventually done the trick, but even now, as a middle-aged mother and successful author of unapologetically lurid fiction, Francine Fisk was tempted to pick up a clump of earth, place it on her tongue.

"What's that child doing?" yelled Malcolm.

"Sunbathing," Francine called out.

Her father snorted. "Is she trying to get eaten?" he cried. "Is that girl waiting for someone to come along and stuff her?"

According to the sole interview Darryl Chase Jr. granted before he died by lethal injection in the fall of 1997, the only human beings he'd ever stuffed and mounted were his father and his brother. Knowing that such things would be frowned upon not only by his wife and stepson but also by society at large, he hadn't stashed his family members in the cellar for ease of communing, à la Norman Bates, but had elected instead to bury them in the backyard. After reading this interview and Sid Chase's posthumously published memoir, *Boyhood, Broken*, Francine had known that she would tell Darryl's story.

She'd tried again and again, for months, to start the book, but her attempts had all failed. Then her best friend from college, an editor who'd fled the New York grind for Chapel Hill five years earlier, had seen in the paper a notice about the auction of Darryl Chase's house and property. Apparently Chase's stepson, Spencer, had a problem with methamphetamine and was unable to keep up with the tax payments. It was around this time that Francine's father suffered a breakdown and came to live with her and Eva, and the sudden availability of the Chase property had seemed like a benediction. A place of convalescence for Malcolm; a way to remove Eva from the dangers of the city, the seamy underbelly of which the child would discover soon enough; but most important, an inhabitable map of the mind of Darryl Chase.

Even in his home, however, even seated in the studio in which he skinned his father and brother, in which he shaved and molded polyurethane foam to resemble their torsos, noses, and limbs, Francine had been getting nowhere. It occurred to her more than once that she might glean inspiration from Darryl Chase's work. It would behoove her, she thought, to discover a hidden cache of the man's mounted animals. She imagined herself stumbling upon a secret passage, uncovering a trophy room filled with owls and moose, deer and bears, badgers and bloodhounds and foxes. To keep himself in crystal meth, however, Spencer Chase had long since sold all his stepfather's creations, so Francine seemed to be out of luck.

She sat back on her heels, put down her spade, glanced around the backyard. Eva lay prone, her skin pinking in the sun. Francine wondered if her daughter had drifted off. Francine turned to the southeast. She studied her increasingly frail father. Malcolm sat erect, but his eyes were closed. He still gripped a paintbrush in his knotty right hand, which had fallen by his side. He wasn't moving. As she wondered whether her father was even breathing, there descended on Francine Fisk a remarkable contentment. This feeling was clean. It was quiet. It hardly registered, however, for the feeling was eclipsed, almost instantly, by a tide of panic. Francine's heart began to kick at her rib cage.

"Dad?" she called across the yard. "Dad!"

Malcolm shook his white head, as if coming out of a fog. He cleared his throat. "Yes?"

"You hungry?" said Francine. "It must be lunchtime."

"Franny," said Malcolm, "can you ever forgive me?"

"For what?"

Malcolm shrugged. "Those things I did to you."

"Oh, Dad," Francine said. "Never mind."

"*I'm* hungry," said Eva, who'd flipped over and now sat Indian style on her towel. "To tell you the truth, I'm starved!"

"Help your grandfather get his things inside," Francine said, "and don't let him carry that easel alone. I'll be there in a minute. How does turkey on rye sound? With avocado? And I think there's fruit salad."

Eva and Malcolm vanished inside. Francine was about to rise, to follow her family, but she felt compelled once again to pick up her spade. She turned over the dark, delicious earth twice, and that was when she saw it, staring up at her from the dirt. Pink, hairless, and wrinkled, with tiny eyes, wide-open mouth boasting four large, dirty-yellow incisors. Briefly, Francine thought the creature was still living. That it had just tunneled its way up. She kept digging gently around the artifact, freed it from the soil, lifted it clear. The mounted animal stood upright on a block of wood, its teeth bared as if ready to do battle, an attitude Francine would describe, in the book, as one of "eternal ferocity."

I know what you did. You can't hide it.

Francine had shaped her first racy best seller around an

incestuously entangled father and daughter. After the book's release, her father hadn't spoken to her for three years. Then Malcolm suffered his breakdown, and he repeatedly cited remorse as its root cause. And no matter how many times Francine attempted to convince her father that the book had been a work of fiction, she was unable to disabuse the old man of his persistent guilty notions.

"Your mind," Malcolm kept saying, "is repressing the memories. In order to spare you. Someday the dam will break and those memories will well up, rise to the surface. Saturate you. Someday, those memories will drown you."

You'll never bury it deep enough. Someone's going to dig it up.

Once the wrinkled pink relic had been safely submerged, folded back into the bosom of the earth, Francine joined her family inside. After lunch, she rubbed aloe into Eva's sun-kissed skin. She tucked an afghan around Malcolm, who'd fallen asleep on the couch, pecked the old man's mottled cheek. Francine then retired to the taxidermy studio of Darryl Chase Jr., the man who'd claimed, just before his execution, that he had the right to kill and mount his father and brother because of the blood that bound them. "Blood ties," he'd said, "grant one permission and absolution." Francine understood this. She understood far more about Darryl than it would ever be safe to let on. The book she would write about him would become her greatest triumph, and she was happy to sit very still, in the midst of his native habitat, endeavoring to channel Darryl Chase, waiting for inspiration to strike.

Hobbled

The jay slices through your field of vision, bearing in her beak something squirmy to deliver to her nestlings, which hatched while you and Shane were barricaded in the house, blinds drawn, gripping plucked toilet paper tubes, chasing acrid plumes of smoke rising from aluminum foil squares, wondering who might be crouched in the overgrown azaleas, whether life exists on other planets, whether anyone else ever laughed so hard, which country artist might record your song. Shane stole the melody from the jay that built her nest in the crab apple outside Nadine's ramshackle bungalow, but when you point this out, he flies into a fury. Smashes his guitar, the acoustic Martin that belonged to his father, who roadied for Bocephus and came within a whisker of making it in Nashville. Seizes your slight shoulders, shakes you until your head lolls, until you see nothing but whipping lengths of unwashed hair and streaks of Shane—his straight, yellowing teeth, his etched brow. He slaps you twice, then withdraws to a corner to crouch, rock, and weep. You sink to the carpet and sit cross-legged, thinking how Nadine's previous boyfriends would have bloodied you for half as much—the Hell's Angel from Sarasota, the construction foreman from Bristol. *Pussy*, you say to Shane, but gently, and when he ventures out for more baking soda you perch backward on the sofa, blinds twisted open, begging Claxton Road for a glimpse of his returning pickup. He's been off and on with

Nadine since you were fourteen, and like the others he's stupid, but unlike them he's tender. Cries like a child at the sight of anything crippled, broken, lame. He's never fucked you—not even when Nadine's passed out or missing in action, as she's been now for a week, not even when you've stripped for him, ground your downy crotch into his thigh, pleaded. He kisses the nape of your neck. Pulls you into his lap. Cradles you. Listens. As light soaks the firmament, you abandon the sofa, open the front door, penetrate the mist that cloaks the weedy yard, shimmy up the crab apple's rough trunk. You wear the red bra and purple panties you've had on for days, since Shane materialized on the porch, a glint in his eye, two eight balls stashed in his Jaguars windbreaker. You locate the nest, study the baby jays—five yellow beaks yawning like forsythia in bloom; membranous lids taut over bulgy eyes; flesh-toned, vein-mapped things awash in damp fuzz and blue-specked shell fragments. When Shane finds you there, when he discovers that you've methodically, tenderly, snapped one of each chick's tiny wings, he'll tear at his hair, tears sliding down his sun-browned cheeks. *Why?* he'll say. *My God, Talley, why?* But it won't be possible to explain to him that you couldn't let the birds go. That if they flew away, they would take with them all that was left of your heart.

Options Counseling

"I saw them this morning," you say, "when I was coming home from the gym."

"Who?"

"The people in my apartment."

"You came home from the gym and found people in your apartment?"

"No." You seize a pen, click it twice. A point peeks from its shaft, retreats. "It just looked that way."

The pressed wood table before you offers up a series of informational pages. The eyes of the young man seated across from you are blue. He was probably born right around the time you were mastering masturbation with Jenny Benz, humping life-size dolls in her bedroom closet while her parents were at work, until you were racked by little-girl orgasms. Or perhaps he sallied forth from his mother's womb the very night Kenneth Parker drilled through your hymen in the backseat of his father's Skylark. The young man studies you, folds his hands on the table. "I'm afraid I don't understand," he says.

"I live alone in a garage apartment," you say, "at the end of a long drive. For four weeks, or perhaps it's been five, each time I pull into the drive in daylight, I glance up at my apartment and think I see, through the front windows, people moving around inside."

"Creepy," says the young man. "When you go in, what do you find?"

"Nothing," you say. "My empty apartment, just as I left it."

He cocks his head.

"I've considered the possibility," you say, "that the people I see are the shades of former tenants. That, unwilling or unable to vacate the premises, they're free to roam about only in my absence. Or perhaps they're always there but only visible to me once I've gone and come back. The way a smell tends, when one enters a room, to strike one, then fades."

The young man sits in silence. The scar that bisects his right eyebrow reminds you of your first kiss, Hal Forrester, who took a wayward bat to the forehead during a third-grade softball game. In first grade, when Mrs. Norton asked you to tell the class what you wanted to be when you grew up, Hal Forrester said "Astronaut." You said "Mother."

"Soon," you tell the young man, "I became convinced that each time I exited my apartment I left behind echoes of my physical self. And that what I saw in the windows on my return was that which would confront anyone who decided to spy on me. A moving picture of myself executing the tasks of daily life. Something slow moving, contemplative, allegorical. Shot in black-and-white."

The young man nods, gently.

"But I think the real explanation," you say, "is that my apartment was built at the convergence of a cluster of parallel universes, and what I see when I approach my home, even after a brief absence, are projected images of a life I might now be living if, at a crucial moment in my past, I'd ignored my instincts. Touched off a wholly divergent chain of events. As I climb the stairs, as I joggle my key in the dead bolt, I find myself hoping that there's been a cosmic mix-up. That somehow I've crossed from our universe into another. That what waits for me inside aren't shades or echoes but children. A husband. A family."

The young man smiles with devastating kindness. He reaches across the table, smothers your hand with a velvety palm. You wonder how many hours he spent in front of a mirror, perfecting this consummate mask of compassion. "I know it's difficult," he says, "but this is *your* decision. Don't let anyone pressure you into doing something that's not right for you."

Behind his head hangs a poster: a colossal, varicolored diagram of the female reproductive system. The uterus is orange. The ovaries are purple. The fallopian tubes are pink. You squint and you think you spy a white speck traveling down the left-hand tube. This is probably a trick of the fluorescent lighting. The young man's hair is cut into a short, neatly trimmed, entirely unexpected Mohawk. You wonder what his parents think.

"Ms. Frost," he says, "you're just six weeks along. There's still plenty of time."

You study the papers before you. Small black letters march across, forming words, phrases, sentences, spelling out options. You know this young man is accustomed to counseling women two decades younger than yourself, girls who *do* have time. Time to plan and create the lives they'd like to live. You want to ask him how anyone can know whether a decision will, in the end, be right for them. To ask if he can carry within himself two conflicting viewpoints and still function. To ask if it might be possible to expunge all your options but one, since you are, and always have been, paralyzed by choice. But you know asking these questions would be futile. The young man is not trained to field such queries. He is trained only to give an overview. To spout empathy by rote. To provide alternatives, but no relief. You know that the gulf dividing one person from another is too wide, too deep for anyone to ford. That the meaningful struggles of humankind are fought not within the frame of the Big Picture but in the winding pathways of the viscera. In the chambers of the heart.

"What do you imagine," you say, "it is that I see? When I stand outside my apartment, looking in?"

The young man creases his forehead. He props his chin on a fist. The two of you sit in silence as he gropes for an answer you know he will not find.

Double Helix

He'd been caught off guard by it, the diminutiveness of what she required. Which isn't to say he hadn't grasped the fact that she would be small. He saw what was implied by the furnishings with which they'd stocked the nursery, the clothing that distant cousins and the wives of college buddies had sent in bright packages, the tiny spoon with which they'd shoveled strained carrots into the soft hollow of her mouth. But he himself was a big man—six five in dress socks and no longer the beanpole he'd been until he turned thirty. For a decade plus one annum, flesh had been marching on his midsection, anchoring him to earth—giving him a structural quality, like a building or a retaining wall. Eleanor had remarked on this more than once as she'd climbed the scaffolding of his frame, searching always for purchase. So it was little wonder that the baby things he and Celeste gathered before Penelope's birth had seemed so minuscule, but where in God's name had he gotten the impression that what they were expecting was impervious to injury, not a living thing but an infant-size doll?

"Dr. Gilbert?"

Mitch looked up. Prosecuting Attorney Blake Huntress blinked at him expectantly, blond eyebrows raised, sheen of perspiration glinting on upper lip.

"I'm sorry," Mitch said. "What was the question?"

"I asked," said PA Huntress, glancing around the courtroom,

"Dr. Gilbert, if you would explain to the court the nature of your relationship with Eleanor Frost."

"She was one of my students."

"And what," said PA Huntress, "was the nature of the course in which she was enrolled?"

"A biology lecture," said Mitch, "called Signs of Life. We study the primary literature of genetics. Starting with Darwin and Mendel. Ending with Jim Watson."

"How many students," said PA Huntress, turning away from Mitch, walking toward the jury box, clasping his hands behind his back, "were enrolled in this lecture?"

"Two hundred and ninety."

"So is it safe to say," said PA Huntress, "that in teaching such a course you don't have personal contact with many of your students?"

Mitch nodded. "Most of them."

"Dr. Gilbert." PA Huntress studied the jury forewoman, a sharp-eyed grandmother of nine who would spend the entirety of Eleanor Frost's manslaughter trial knitting, her needles furiously flying, a blur. As an undergrad, PA Huntress had been one course shy of a lit minor and something of a fool for Dickens, for the Victorians in toto, and he privately referred to this obsessive knitter as "Madame Defarge." The unceasing clack of her needles reminded him of a model train careening along its tracks, in danger of derailing. The sound would haunt him for the trial's duration, throbbing through his nights, a sleepy undercurrent, and during the day PA Huntress would at times be forced to shout in order to drown it out. By trial's end, the purple scarf on which Mme. Defarge was working would be far too long to wrap around the neck of any one human being, and PA Huntress kept wondering what sort of mob she might be planning to yoke together with it. “Did you have personal contact with Eleanor Frost?”

She’d been one of nearly two hundred girls enrolled in Signs of Life—the second of a two-part sequence for nonmajors that fulfilled the university’s science requirement—nearly two hundred girls for whom the eight a.m. time slot made rolling out of bed and sprinting to class a necessity, two hundred girls in pajama bottoms and slouchy boots, two hundred girls with hair tugged back into ponytails or up into topknots. Mitch couldn’t remember the first time he’d noticed Eleanor. She’d sat always in the northeast quadrant of the lecture hall, but this was something he would only become aware of once their joint evolution had begun.

“She came to my office hours a couple of times,” Mitch said, staring at PA Huntress’s pinstriped back. “Eleanor had questions about the physical structure of DNA. About how heritable traits are encoded within it.”

“And what,” said PA Huntress, “did you tell her?”

“That DNA resembles a twisted ladder. Its rails are phosphate–sugar chains, and paired nitrogenous bases joined by hydrogen bonds make up its rungs. Of the four different bases—A, C, G, and T—A can pair only with T, and C can connect only with G. Like letters that spell out the words that make up a sentence, the sequence of bases in a molecule of DNA specifies, encodes, expresses, and transmits the genetic information that governs every form of life.”

“Dr. Gilbert.” PA Huntress turned away from Mme. Defarge. He scanned the gallery, the back row of which teemed with reporters, journalists waiting to see how Blake Huntress would handle this, the most sensational trial of his career to date, a trial that happened to be taking place during an election year.

PA Huntress rested a hand on the jury box rail. He let his gaze alight, briefly, on Judge Bartholomew Mortimer before pinning it to Eleanor Frost, who sat beside Beverly Angelopoulos, her famously desirable defense attorney. "Were these visits to office hours your sole personal contact with Ms. Frost?"

Mitch nodded. "Yes."

"Do you have any notion," said PA Huntress, moving toward the defense table, taking note of Eleanor's ivory skin, slender crossed arms, tumult of black curls, enormous eyes, the hue of which Alfred (Lord) Tennyson might have likened to a summer sky about to spawn a tempest or to algae obliterating the surface of a pond, "of why Ms. Frost would wish to harm your family?"

Even the way he shook his head, even the way he denied her, made Eleanor's heart throb, seize, gallop. She had only to lower her lids to find herself alone with Mitch in his office, door locked, shades drawn, her forehead and fingertips pressed lightly to his. She'd gone to see him that first day about his lectures. About notions he'd put forth that were distressing Eleanor. Ideas that were invading her dreams. Disturbing her previously undisturbed slumber.

"Each of you," Mitch had said as he paced before the board, hands in pockets, white streak of chalk dust on left pant leg, "was mapped out at the moment of your conception. When your father's sperm broke through your mother's egg wall, *you* were determined, in your entirety. The color of your eyes. Whether you'll develop bipolar disorder or bunions. Whether you'll grow fat and have a violent temper. Whether you'll be an artist or an alcoholic. And the tale told by your DNA's text is fixed. Immutable." Mitch paused at the lectern, studied the sleepy students. "It's even determined, in the first instant of your existence, precisely how and when you will die."

"I don't think," said Eleanor, "that you can go around saying things like that."

"Like what?"

"That your whole life is encoded in your DNA. That everything that's going to happen is fixed from the moment you're born. Some of the things you said in class are wildly inaccurate. They go against the accepted tenets of modern genetic theory, which recognizes the undeniable influence of environment."

"What's your name?"

"Eleanor Frost."

She stood before his desk, a girl not unlike the others, wearing pajama bottoms, black curls wrangled into a haphazard topknot. There was something about Eleanor's face—the distance between her eyes, eyes whose color would confound Mitch until he woke one morning two weeks later whispering the words *blue spruce,* or that which lay between her eyes and the dark brows arching over them—that made her look perpetually startled. As though every moment of her life were unexpected. A revelation.

"I've been teaching biology," Mitch said, "for thirteen years, Ms. Frost. I have a PhD. Are you trying to tell me that I don't know what I'm talking about?"

"No," said Eleanor. "No, of course not."

Mitch rose, circumambulated his desk. As he took up a position that could be construed as too close to Eleanor Frost, he realized something was wrong with his lungs. It was as though he'd been breathing a certain way for forty-one years, since he'd gushed from Geraldine Gilbert's womb, slick with blood and fluids, and that here, now, in his office, towering over this unknown girl, this unknown variable, his respiratory system were undergoing a recalibration. Which could, perhaps, account for his light-headedness.

"It just seems irresponsible," Eleanor said, "to present a one-sided view of something so important. To not acknowledge that this stuff is debatable."

"Most people your age," said Mitch, "aren't all that concerned with responsibility."

Eleanor nodded.

"Do you think environment plays a larger role than biology? In the person one turns out to be?"

Eleanor shrugged.

"Have you ever considered the possibility," said Mitch, "that even ways in which people are changed by their environment might be determined ahead of time? That our genes might encode even those things that seem like random, accidental, unpredictable events?"

Eleanor shook her head.

"How does that make you feel, Ms. Frost?"

Eleanor flushed. She pulled her hands inside the sleeves of her hoodie, wrapped her arms around her shoulders, studied the waxed floor. "Frightened," she said.

"Why?"

"Because if everything's already been decided," said Eleanor, "I can't see the point in living."

Unreasonably, embarrassingly, she started crying and attempted to bolt. In three strides, Mitch crossed the room and caught her by the wrist at the door. The look on his face—forehead creased, eyebrows slanted like forward slash, backslash, lips moist and slightly parted, eyes glimmering as if with unshed tears—made Eleanor yearn to clamber inside his rib cage, to fit her slight frame within his, like a nesting doll, like Mitch's own daughter must once have been hidden when she was still a germ, a seed, a notion, secreted inside him. Mitch had spoken in class of his six-year-old daughter, Penelope, a child named by Mitch's wife, who taught in the Classics department, for the resourceful wife of Odysseus.

Eleanor pressed herself into Mitch, began climbing his frame, at which point Mitch sat on a chair, tugged her into his lap. He kissed her experimentally, provisionally, then with escalating hunger, and even as their chins slickened with saliva, even as Eleanor sloughed off her hoodie and pajama bottoms, even as Mitch held her aloft to nuzzle her abdomen, he kept saying things like *I can't do this. I've never done anything like this. What am I doing? Why am I doing this?*

"We couldn't figure out what she was doing," Reginald Tarkington said from the witness stand, "Gloria and me."

"And who," said PA Huntress, "is Gloria?"

"My wife." Reginald indicated a woman seated behind the prosecution table, not far from Mitchell Gilbert. Grinning madly, Gloria Tarkington fluffed her peroxide hair. Her chins rippled as she waved at PA Huntress, who returned the gesture with a weak flap of his left hand. "She'd had an appointment at the Holistic Healing Center—twice a week Gloria gets acupuncture for her sciatica. I have to drive her because afterward she's woozy. Anyway, we were traveling north on Avondale, and as we approached the intersection of Avondale and Centurion, we noticed the Skylark."

"The Skylark?" On this, day five of the trial, Blake Huntress was handicapped. The night before, he'd allowed the junior prosecutors to goad him into going out to the Silver Chalice, where he'd ended up drinking twelve tequila shooters, pulling a pair of panty hose over his head, and climbing upon a table to recite Robert Browning's "My Last Duchess." *How in hell is it,* he wondered, as he made a circuit of the courtroom, as he drew near the jury box, *that I'm still so susceptible to peer pressure?* His head pounding in rhythm with Mme. Defarge's clacking needles, he wondered, not for the first time, how the woman avoided errors, since she never seemed to look down at her work.

"It was a blue Skylark," said Reginald Tarkington, "probably four years old, and it was traveling in the middle lane on Avondale. Not the left turn lane, you understand, but the one in the middle. Gloria and me, we were traveling in the right-hand lane when the light turned red, and we came to a stop beside this Skylark. Funny thing was, the driver had left about two car lengths between herself and the vehicle in front of her, which was the first car at the light. A silver compact, some Honda, Toyota, Nissan. Anyway, Gloria and I started commenting on the amount of room the driver of the Skylark had left, because it just seemed so unusual."

"What time of day was this?" said PA Huntress.

"Ten to five."

"So there was a good bit of traffic. Rush hour, is that correct?"

"Oh, yes. Heavy traffic."

"Mr. Tarkington," said PA Huntress, "can you identify the driver of the Skylark?"

Reginald shoved his bifocals up the bridge of his nose with a crooked finger. He then pointed that same digit at Eleanor Frost, who sat at the defense table next to Beverly Angelopoulos, whose comely face, PA Huntress was sure, could launch far more than a thousand ships. "That's her."

"Let the record show," said PA Huntress, "that the witness has indicated the defendant, Eleanor Frost. Now, Mr. Tarkington, did you notice anything else about Ms. Frost? Besides how much room she'd left between her car and the silver compact?"

"Well." Reginald glanced at Gloria, who was nodding and

giving him the thumbs-up sign with both hands. "I don't like to be nosy, but we *were* curious, just because of how much room she'd left, so we were looking at her."

"What did you see?"

"She was very young. And she seemed to be upset. Distressed. She was definitely crying, and she was talking to herself, and she would sometimes touch her head like it was paining her."

"Thank you, Mr. Tarkington. Would you please tell the court what happened next?"

Reginald nodded. "Gloria and I were talking about her mother, my mother-in-law, Bernice, who was coming to stay the following week, and our conversation was getting a bit heated, when we heard a car peel out. We looked left just in time to see the Skylark ram the silver compact. The collision pushed the compact right out into the traffic along Centurion. Gloria grabbed my wrist and was hollering, *Do something, Reggie! We've got to do something!* But there wasn't anything to be done. The compact was struck over and over, first by a westbound car, then an eastbound car, then another westbound car, and so on. That poor car looked like a leaf or a twig, something terribly light, being manhandled by a stiff wind."

"Mr. Tarkington," said PA Huntress, dropping his voice, approaching the witness stand, wishing he'd thought to pop a Tylenol before he'd passed out the night before, wondering when his mouth would stop tasting like a litter box, "would you please tell the court what you saw next?"

Reginald looked to Gloria, who'd pulled a lace-edged handkerchief from her quilted handbag and was now sobbing into it, occasionally blowing her nose. PA Huntress couldn't decide whether the sound reminded him more of a trumpet blast or the honk of a goose.

"It was awful," said Reginald. "The most awful thing I've ever seen."

"Go on," said PA Huntress.

"The fifth time the silver compact was hit, or maybe it was the sixth—everything happened so fast, you know, it's tough to say—something came flying up out of the car. Through the windshield. It was like someone had heaved it. Or like it had been launched, like there was a catapult in the passenger seat. Something small and spindly came up and out of that car, smashed right through the windshield, and it was a minute before Gloria and I understood that it was a child."

"A child?"

"Yes," said Reginald, wiping roughly at his eyes. "A little girl. With blond hair. The even more horrifying thing, and Gloria will back me up on this, is that she seemed to hang there, suspended over the intersection, for far longer than is physically possible. When she finally fell, she lay there, her limbs all folded the wrong way, her neck twisted, and I thought, *It's a doll. Please God let it be a doll.* I don't know how many cars ran over the poor thing. I . . . I just don't know."

"I don't know," Eleanor had said to the nurse practitioner she saw at University Health Services the day before the police showed up at the front door of her parents' redbrick American Foursquare. The nurse practitioner, a heavyset woman with a steel-gray bob, stood before Eleanor, who was dressed in a paper gown and seated on the edge of an exam table. The NP kept looking from Eleanor's face to Eleanor's chart, which she held in her left hand.

"You don't have any idea," said the NP.

Eleanor shook her head.

"You can't even guess," said the NP, "who might have fathered this child."

Eleanor shook her head again. "No," she said. "I can't."

Three days earlier, she'd lain facing Mitch on the blue couch in his office, their legs stacked like Lincoln Logs, notched at the knee, listening to him talk about his family, about the complexity of his feelings for them. "Do I love them?" he'd asked. Eleanor had grown used to his habit of asking questions only he could answer. "I do," he continued, "very much. I've never felt dissatisfied with my home life. I am of course not entirely content—who is—and at times, yes, I wish I could go back. Start over. Who doesn't? Celeste is a breathtaking woman. She's witty and brilliant. Penelope is a good girl. And beautiful. Well, she's the mirror image of her mother. I must admit, however, that at times I look at the two of them and wonder what the fuck I'm doing here. Living under the same roof with these people. Sharing a bed with my own wife. Are we truly connected, and how? Do I really know them? Do they know me? Do they *want* to know me? Is it possible, at this point, for us to evolve? Or have we become brittle, calcified, frozen into our various roles—*father, mother, daughter, husband, wife*? Are people capable of a different kind of connection, one that requires no label? An association so primal, so profound, so fundamental, that no one word can contain it? A symbiotic relationship as necessary to sense-making and survival as the pairing of DNA's four bases? A to T, C to G, G to C, T to A?"

When they lay piled together on the blue couch, Eleanor was forced to tilt back her head to see Mitch's face. From this angle, his forehead was as remote as Alaska, his chin a jutting Gulf Coast peninsula. Mitch's nose had been badly broken when he was eleven, in an automobile accident that claimed his mother's life. Minutes after picking him up from school on a Friday, Geraldine Gilbert ran a red light, at which time a speeding pickup plowed into the driver's side of her Buick

Century. Mitch's misaligned nose made him look more rugged than he actually was and contrasted sharply with his wire-rimmed glasses. Whenever they started fooling around, Mitch would remove his spectacles, which pleased Eleanor, who detested the way their frames masked the size and warmth of his brown eyes. Afterward Mitch could never find his glasses, and sometimes, once they'd dressed and were turning the office upside down, Eleanor would spot them but say nothing, to enjoy for a bit longer the sight of Mitch's eyes. If she didn't tilt back her head, however, as they lay on the blue couch, she would study Mitch's chest—a vaguely centerline spot beneath which her recent exhaustive studies of human anatomy had told her his heart must lie. Eleanor liked to imagine his skin and tissue dissolving, as well as his muscle and bone, to create a hollow for his heart. She imagined herself reaching into this crater, plucking out the fist-size organ, cradling it in her palm. Kissing it. Baring her teeth. Sinking them into Mitch's heart as though it were an overripe fruit.

"Eleanor," Mitch said, "we're going away soon."

"We?" Eleanor tilted back her head.

"My family," said Mitch. "We're going to Maine. We summer there. With Celeste's parents."

"Can't they go without you?" Eleanor said. "Can't you stay behind?"

"No," Mitch said. "No, I don't see how that would work."

Eleanor reconsidered the suffocating trio of months that stretched out before her. Her father, a mild-mannered and nearly transparent CPA, was expecting her to work in his office and to spend time with her grandmother, who had dementia and lived in a continuing care facility. Eleanor's mother was expecting Eleanor to accompany her to the neighborhood pool and rub sunscreen into her broadening, freckling back. To listen to her bitch about her husband, about how he didn't appreciate her, how he couldn't understand how lucky he was, how good he had it. She was expecting Eleanor to scrape her off the floor each night, once she'd lost count of her vodka gimlets, to undress her and put her to bed in the room she hadn't shared with her husband for a decade, to tuck her in, kiss her forehead, whisper "Good night."

"I know." Eleanor sat up on the blue couch in Mitch's office. "I could come to Maine with you. Be Penelope's nanny."

Mitch smiled, but he shook his head. "It's just not possible."

Eleanor stood, retrieved her shed clothing from a colorful area rug Celeste Gilbert had purchased for pennies at a market in Morocco, while she and Mitch were there on honeymoon.

"Don't be angry," Mitch said. "Eleanor."

Eleanor said nothing. She started jerking on her clothes.

"Look," Mitch said, "if it weren't for Penelope, I would stay. I promise."

PA Blake Huntress woke on day seven of Eleanor Frost's trial to find the morning pregnant with promise. Since he'd entered what he could no longer deny was his middle age, PA Huntress's hangovers had become two-day affairs, and now that this one had passed, he was gripped by a paranormal sense of hope. A family of birds had taken up residence in the eaves of his home, and though their song generally drove him nuts, this morning they sounded soothing. As he shaved his cheeks and chin, as he brushed the yellow scum from his tongue, PA Huntress imagined that the birds were skylarks. In the mirror he started reciting "The Lark Ascending," by George Meredith, who PA Huntress would for some reason always recall a college professor saying "was dedicated to the idea that life is a process of evolution." Later, in the courtroom, as he watched Eleanor push up from the defense table, distended belly first, and waddle to the witness stand, as he watched Beverly Angelopoulos examine her client, PA Huntress decided that on the way home he would stop at a pet store, pick up a couple of feeders and some birdseed.

Once Beverly had returned to her table, sat, and recrossed her legendary legs, PA Huntress stood. He glanced at the jurors, the spectators, Judge Mortimer. Beverly was good; she'd guided Eleanor through testimony that made it seem all but impossible for the young woman to be held accountable for the deaths of Penelope Gilbert and the three other people who'd died on the afternoon of April 29. PA Huntress sensed a sympathetic vibe seeping through the courtroom, but even this did nothing to dispel his optimism.

"Ms. Frost," he said, "you've testified that you were on your way home from Whispering Rivers, an assisted living facility where you'd gone to visit your grandmother, when you arrived at the intersection of Avondale and Centurion Avenues at ten minutes to five p.m. Is that correct?"

Eleanor nodded. "That's right."

"You've further testified," said PA Huntress, "that your grandmother, who suffers from dementia, had that day, for the first time in weeks, recognized you. That she'd retrieved from a shoe box on a closet shelf a photograph of your parents, a picture you'd never seen, taken not long after your parents met, a photo in which they looked, to quote your earlier testimony, 'ecstatic,' 'joyful,' and 'full of hope.'"

"Yes," said Eleanor. "She said the moment she snapped it she knew my mom and dad were meant to be, that their marriage wasn't choice but necessity. The lens allowed her to see a *biological* component to their attraction. She said their being together wasn't a decision but a fact of life."

"Your grandmother, who often doesn't recognize you, said all this? That is your testimony?"

"Yes."

"And you further testified," said PA Huntress, after pausing for effect, "that this visit caused you a good bit of emotional distress. Once she'd fallen asleep in her recliner, you said, you kissed your grandmother's forehead, walked out to your father's car. And it wasn't until you'd driven six miles, you said, until you found yourself approaching the intersection of Avondale and Centurion, that you realized you'd taken the picture of your parents. That you were still clutching the photo in your hand."

Eleanor nodded. "Yes."

"And you further testified," said PA Huntress, embarking on a circuit of the courtroom, his 263rd of the trial, approaching the jury, watching Mme. Defarge's knotty fingers fly, watching the grandmother's sharp eyes, which were pinned to the pregnant woman in the witness box, "that it was while you attempted to retrieve this photograph, which had slipped from your fingers and fluttered to the floorboard, that your foot slid off the brake pedal and hit the gas, causing your father's Skylark to lurch forward, to slam into the silver Toyota driven by Celeste Gilbert, to send it flying out into traffic."

"Yes," said Eleanor.

"And you say you had no idea," said PA Huntress, drawing near Mme. Defarge, whose frenetic fingers seemed to be calling him, pulling him ever closer, like the song of the Sirens who attempted to lure Odysseus to his doom, "that the Toyota in front of you contained the wife and daughter of your biology professor, Dr. Mitchell Gilbert."

Eleanor shook her head. "None."

"And the only explanation you've offered," said PA Huntress, "for the two car lengths of distance Reginald Tarkington and other witnesses have testified that you left is that your visit with your grandmother had left you in a highly emotional state. You were crying and gasping for air, you said, and you must have misjudged the distance between your car and the car in front of you."

"Yes," said Eleanor. "That's exactly right."

"Well then, Ms. Frost," said PA Huntress, who, to the consternation of Judge Mortimer and Beverly Angelopoulos, to the bewilderment of the journalists seated in the gallery, to the confusion of Reginald and Gloria Tarkington, of Dr. Mitchell Gilbert and the rest of the assembly, had dropped to his knees and seemed to be genuflecting in front of the jury's knitting forewoman, "I have only one further question. What became of the photograph?"

"I'm sorry?"

"The black-and-white photograph of your parents you inadvertently stole from your grandmother and were straining to reach when your foot hit the gas pedal, causing this horrifying traffic accident, an accident that stole four human lives and left five other people, including Celeste Gilbert, permanently disabled. Police officers and emergency personnel made a thorough search of the scene, including the interior of your father's car, and no photograph was ever found. Can you explain this to the court, please, Ms. Frost?"

"Why?" Mitch had said when, against the advice of friends, family, and counsel, he'd gone to see Eleanor in jail. Pressing to his ear the handset of the phone through which they were forced to speak, he viewed his former student through glass threaded with metallic wire, studied her pale, stormy-eyed, startled face, the profusion of uncut curls springing from her scalp. "Eleanor. Why?"

"Mitch." Eleanor touched her belly, which had not yet begun to burgeon. "You can't believe that I meant for any of this to happen."

Mitch removed his wire-rimmed spectacles, dropped them on the counter. He closed his eyes, pressed thumb and forefinger into his lids. He was unshaven, unshowered. He wore a threadbare flannel over a stained T-shirt, clothing Eleanor had never seen. Sitting slumped and filthy, without his glasses, with his crooked nose and his hidden eyes, Mitch didn't seem to be the same man with whom Eleanor had lain on the blue couch, the man to whom she'd felt so close, the man whose heart she'd fantasized about removing and consuming. Trepidation thrummed, momentarily, through Eleanor; it wouldn't occur to her until much later that her sudden apprehension and discomfort probably had to do with perspective. That one grows accustomed to viewing things from a certain angle. That even the very familiar can appear to be foreign when viewed head-on.

"Are you saying," said Mitch, "that your actions weren't premeditated? That you aren't responsible for what happened?"

"Mitch." Eleanor lifted her left hand, splayed it flat against the safety glass. "Do you remember telling me that even the ways in which people adapt to their environment might be determined ahead of time? That our genes could encode even those things that seem like random, accidental, unpredictable events?"

Mitch nodded.

"Responsibility," said Eleanor, "is something to which we sentence ourselves."

Mitch retrieved his glasses from the counter. He fitted them over his eyes.

"Natural selection," said Eleanor, "is unavoidable. What matters is adaptation. What matters is survival."

Eventually, Mitch raised his right hand and pressed it to the threaded glass, where it dwarfed Eleanor's hand. Threatened to swallow it.

"I ate it," Eleanor said to Judge Bartholomew Mortimer, to those gathered in the courtroom, in response to PA Huntress's question.

"You ate it?" PA Huntress pushed up from the kneeling position he'd assumed, brushed dust from his pinstriped trousers. "The photograph?"

Eleanor nodded. "In that picture, my parents were full of hope. Their love was inevitable. Things had not yet been determined. They had no idea what was to come. I wanted to carry that image with me always. So I tore it into pieces. And I ate it."

"You ate it." Having been deserted, quite suddenly, by the optimism that had been buoying him since he woke, PA Huntress crept back to the prosecution table, slumped into his seat. Not even the warmth of Beverly Angelopoulos's hand on his shoulder, not even her dazzling, sympathetic smile, not even ducking, with this Helen of Defense Attorneys, into a courthouse broom closet and making love amid stained buckets and hanging feather dusters, Beverly's flawless backside balanced over the mop sink, on a low shelf from which PA Huntress had swept spray bottles of Windex and cardboard cylinders of Comet, not even achieving a climax such as he hadn't known since his college days, since he'd first been caught off guard by the sprung rhythms of Gerard Manley Hopkins, could lift Blake Huntress's spirits now. "No further questions, Your Honor."

Six years later, when she would wake from the dream, heart thudding, Eleanor Gilbert would rise from her marriage bed and steal down the hall. She would enter the room of her son, Charlie, named for Charles Darwin, celebrated naturalist, onetime passenger on the HMS *Beagle*. Eleanor would drop to her knees beside her son's bed, touch his cheek. Upon finding his skin to be warm and pliable, she would weep with relief. She would leave Charlie, journey back to the master bedroom. There, before climbing into bed with Mitch, she would enter the closet, reach for the top shelf. From a certain shoebox, Eleanor would extract a handmade scarf, purple in hue and absurdly long. She would sit in a rocker positioned before a bay window, twist the scarf around her neck and, in the moon's anemic glow, study its perfectly formed, evenly spaced stitches.

"Here," Matilda Dandridge had said as she handed Eleanor the scarf, mere moments after she rose from her customary seat in the jury box to pronounce the words *Not guilty*. "This belongs to you, my dear. Its stitches spell out your fate. The things that have happened, as well as those that have yet to come. The entirety of your existence."

"It's hard to believe," Mitch would say later, "that that nutty old bird got through voir dire. Makes you wonder how many juries out there, at this very moment, are stocked with the mentally unstable."

But when he would wake in the still of night to find Eleanor missing from their bed, when he would lift his head and spy his second wife, the woman he married two years after she was exonerated, one year after Celeste divorced him and moved to Maine to live with her parents, sitting at the window in the moon's pale fire, her back hunched, the scarf wound round her neck, her spruce-colored eyes gliding over its stitches, straining to interpret its intelligence, he would not be able to dismiss Matilda Dandridge so easily. Inevitably, Mitch would see the old woman's scarf as a strand of DNA. A double helix. It would occur to him that what strands of genetic information, and purportedly fate-laced scarves, and sentences containing words and phrases revealed was eternally open to interpretation. Just as is this:

Eleanor's recurring nightmare, in which she enters Charlie's room and touches his cheek to find it hard, waxy, cold. She turns him over and discovers that Charlie isn't a boy but a doll: their son is made of molded plastic, the kind that's hollow inside. She is unable to find a single sign of life.

And before Mitch rises, before he crosses the room and kneels before her, before he gently untwists the scarf from around her neck, before he lifts her, carries her to bed, before he sinks down beside her, envelops her with his bulk, before he tries to stem her tears by speaking about the inevitability of evolution, by saying that at times lying is the way to reveal truth, that often the way to preserve a thing is to destroy it, that the sins of the father won't necessarily be visited on the son, before he sings a sequence of nitrogenous DNA bases into her ear—A-T, G-C, C-G, T-A, G-C, A-T—a lullaby that will dissolve into a sequence involving only the first letters of their two names—E-M, M-E, M-E, E-M, E-M, M-E—Mitch will consider what he might find, were he to punch a hole through Eleanor's abdomen. Were he to slice her open, explore the contents of her stomach. Some nights, such thinking will send him into paroxysms of guilt. But on other nights he will manage to convince himself that, were he to root around inside his second wife, he would find, concealed there, Eleanor's own parents.

Or at least a black-and-white photograph of them, miraculously undigested. Harold and Sadie Frost. Two broadly smiling teenagers, skins tanned, thighs just touching, seated on Harold's mother's porch swing on a summer evening, having just met. A couple on the cusp of everything and on the cusp of nothing. A pair twisted inevitably into an association that defies terminology. Conjoined for all time.

By the Numbers

Fifty-one days ago, when the men boarded the eighty-foot yacht on which my father served as first mate for two decades, I was not yet a killer. The *Seas the Day* had been chartered by Mort and Sylvia Stein, of Great Neck, for a three-month cruise they'd planned, for five years, to take with their two grandchildren, Patty and Sam. I once asked my father how best to describe the children of the wealthy and he suggested the word *insufferable*. He also told me seven days was the longest he knew of a person surviving without potable water. He was forty-six years old when the men killed him in front of me, slit his throat with a machete. One of the men held my elbows behind my back, so I couldn't go to him, could give him no comfort. My father hated his name, which was Alfred, so everyone called him Skipper. The last thing he said was "Hard to starboard." Patty Stein, who is three years older than I, lost her virginity beneath her high school's bleachers to a boy on the football team. Number thirty-seven. If Sylvia Stein had been ten years younger, the men might have spared her, like they spared Patty and me, but Sylvia was seventy and she was no good for raping, so they shot her in the stomach and left her on the upper deck, dragging around in small circles, yowling like a cat in heat. It took her two days to bleed to death. One night three weeks after the men boarded the *Seas the Day*, I woke to find myself alone with one of them in a motorboat. We skimmed over an ocean flat as black glass, reflecting a harvest moon. When he cut the engine, the man also cut the twine that bound my wrists and ankles. My father taught me, once, how to crush a trachea with one sharp blow of the elbow. The man was alive but choking when I heaved him overboard, and the compass was still in his pocket. Before his head vanished beneath the wet darkness, he mouthed the words *I love you.* Nearly two weeks ago the boat ran out of gas, and I've yet to see another vessel. I'm twelve years old, and I've been without potable water for six days. The one time I asked my father about my mother he turned away, blinked at the unwavering horizon. "You were born," he told me, "of the sea. My only mistress." I no longer have the strength to sit up, to gaze across the water, but I imagine my mother's eyes—her trillions of eyes—glimmering beneath its surface, searching for me, beckoning me home.

Mastermind

This morning, as my gaze roamed over the assemblage of eye patches, graying temples, prosthetic limbs, and straining waistbands that filled the Central Control Room, I thought of you. Mowing the lawn, driving the station wagon, seated at the head of the dining table. Not that you're anything like them, the aging outlaws who stood around sipping the coffee and nibbling the pastries I'd had flown in from the Professor's favorite Viennese bakery. To the best of my recollection, you never cared for sweets, an attitude you share with Rags Randall, our team's computer and communications expert. Although none of us knows his exact age, it's obvious that Rags is still a child, and when the Professor initially approached me about bringing him into the Organization, I was resistant. Children make me nervous. But the Professor insisted, and though I'd already seen evidence that my mentor's mind was fraying, I obeyed. As I've always obeyed.

"Everyone," I said, checking the time, clapping my hands, "we're at half past seven. Let's take our seats."

It's been nearly a year since our Organization last committed a full-scale global crime or enacted a scene of international terror, and as we settled around the boat-shaped, marble-topped conference table, the air crackled with anticipation.

"By now," I said to the assembly, "all our operatives are in place. They'll start moving on their primary targets in a quarter of an hour."

"Carl," said Beatrice Bot, the infamous Man-Eater of Manchester. The sole woman seated at the conference table, Bea is not only notoriously sensitive about her appearance but also notoriously hungry for the flesh of male humans, and I've never worked up the nerve to ask how in the world she maintains her trademark mustache and goatee. "May I speak freely?"

"Please do," I said.

Bea glanced around the table. Several of our comrades met her gaze and nodded, offering encouragement.

"I'm afraid," said Bea, "that some of us have reservations about Project Rushmore."

"Oh?"

Bea nodded. "It seems, well, rather unlikely that anyone will actually go for it."

Jiang Lau, the Tiny Terror of Taipei, seated across from Bea, spoke animatedly in Chinese for several seconds. The rest of us listened without comprehension and then turned to Bea, who also speaks Chinese.

"Jiang says," said Bea, "that what seems to differentiate this plan from the Professor's former brilliant and diabolical schemes is a certain muddiness of motivation."

"Muddiness," I said.

"You must admit," said Bea, "our goal *is* rather opaque on this one, Carl."

Surveying the room, I spied concern on many of the weathered faces before me. None of our operatives had ever before dared to openly question a plan, decision, or directive of the Professor's, and I wondered if they were starting to catch on to the ways in which our supreme leader was slipping.

Jiang spoke again. We looked to Bea for a translation.

"And some of us," said Bea, lifting both hands to indicate the space in which we were gathered, "have doubts about the volcano."

Recently we relocated from the Philippines to Antarctica, where we excavated an extinct stratovolcano situated some fifty miles inland from the Ross Sea. Inside Mount Overlord, we fabricated an impenetrable, multilevel, state-of-the-art HQ.

"It's perfectly safe," I said. "Mount Overlord last erupted seven million years ago."

Jiang spoke again, repeatedly pounding one small fist against the tabletop.

"Jiang is citing the case," said Bea, "of Mount Saint Helens, another stratovolcano that was thought to be extinct, until it erupted, catastrophically, in May of 1980."

I pushed up to my feet. "Forgive me," I said, "but I'd better find out what's keeping the Professor."

Hurrying over the slate floors of the complex, I mounted stairs, crossed suspension bridges, saluted black-uniformed guards toting automatic weapons. When I reached the Professor's suite, located next to my own, I knocked twice but received no answer. Opening the door and stepping inside, I found that the illumination system was still set to "full night."

"Professor?"

"Is that you, Carl?"

"Yes."

"Is it lunchtime?"

"No, Professor. It's nearly eight a.m. Time for the big meeting, sir."

"Oh."

"Would you like to take a bath? Shall I draw you a bath?"

"No, thank you. I don't much care for dampness."

"Shall I help you up, sir? I could help you dress."

"Carl?"

"Yes?"

"Is it lunchtime?"

"No, Professor."

"Where's Veronica? I'd like to see those tits of hers. I'd like to rest my head on those dirty pillows. Three times I knocked her up, did you know that? But that selfish tramp killed my babies. My children were dead before they got the chance to live."

I didn't bother reminding the Professor that he'd had Veronica Stein killed in the mid-1980s, when he'd discovered that his longtime mistress was sleeping with my predecessor, Mortimer Shaw. Mort and the Professor lived next door to each other as boys, and they'd been building our Organization for more than twenty years the night the Professor had two of his goons toss a live hair dryer into the heart-shaped hot tub in Veronica Stein's penthouse apartment, as Veronica and Mort canoodled within. Afterward, the Professor had the illicit couple hacked into manageable hunks of meat, which he himself hand-fed to Laurel and Hardy, his beloved albino alligators. I've never told a soul how pitifully the Professor wept as he did so.

It was an undeniably tragic business, the matter of Mort and Veronica, but they'd known they were playing with fire. I've often thought the clear and present danger must have greatly heightened the pleasure they derived from their covert liaisons. Others in our Organization have suggested that perhaps the couple grew too comfortable, too complacent, that they forgot how dangerous the Professor can be. Selectivity of memory can be a blessing. Most of the time, however, it's a curse.

"Are you sure?" I said this one year before we set up shop inside Mount Overlord, to Dr. Rahman A. Saleh, as I sat in an exam room opposite the Professor, who was up on one of those upholstered tables covered by a crinkly sheet of white paper. "Is there any way this could be a mistake?"

Dr. Saleh shook his head. "The MRI shows definite brain shrinkage," he said, "and his performance on the memory tests is a clear indication."

The Professor was digging in his trouser pockets. He kept coming up with the same five items: an ancient set of keys that no longer unlock anything, a half-eaten and rewrapped York Peppermint Patty, a roll of quarters, a small piece of paper folded into an even smaller square with one number—313—scribbled on it, and an engraved gold cigarette lighter that the three other charter members of the World Federation of Criminal Masterminds had presented to the Professor on his sixtieth birthday, in recognition of all he's done for the profession. Each time the Professor produced any one of these items, he held it aloft and said, with much pride, "Look!"

"Yes," Dr. Saleh and I took turns saying. "That's very nice. *Very* nice."

"But there must be something we can do," I said to Dr. Saleh. "Some sort of experimental treatment. The Professor is scheduled to speak at a conference in Vienna next month. He's a very important man. And money is no object."

Dr. Saleh crossed his legs. That afternoon the neurologist was wearing a pair of purple and turquoise running sneakers. "How is it," he said, "that you're related to Mr. Smith again?"

"He's my uncle."

"Why do you call him the Professor?"

I shrugged. "Everyone calls him that."

"I cannot imagine," said Dr. Saleh, "that this comes as a surprise. Your uncle's brain function has been deteriorating for quite some time. I'd say he's in the middle stages of the disease.

At this point, his memory loss would be evident to a stranger, let alone to family and friends."

I thought about pointing out to the neurologist that, sometimes, the closer one stands to something the harder it is to see. I first encountered the Professor twenty-five years ago, while working as an adjuster in your insurance office. You remember; this was after I failed out of college for the second time. I'd been on the job nine months when I started waking in the dead of each night, sweating, heart a-hammer. Unable to slide back into slumber, I would roam the streets of our city, and once, before I knew it, I'd snatched the purse that dangled from the shoulder of a woman walking toward me. The act filled me with a cruel mixture of purpose and self-loathing, and a petty crime spree ensued.

After rolling a drunk one night, after striking the grizzled old man repeatedly in the face, I helped him to his feet, dusted him off, apologized, gave him all the money in my pocket. I heard someone laugh and turned to find the Professor seated on a nearby bench, decked out in a camel hair overcoat and fedora. When he stood, I saw that he wasn't as tall as you but was thicker, and more powerfully built. He approached me, wound an arm around my shoulders. His face reminded me of a bulldog's, and he smelled of peppermint and pomade. When he asked if I had a father, I nodded. When he asked if you understood me, I shook my head. *Son,* the Professor said, *I think you're my type. Stick with me. I'll take you places. Show you things.*

"The Professor will be along shortly," I announced at twelve minutes to eight, as I reentered the Central Control Room and took an absurdly high-backed black leather chair at one end of the table. The extravagant furnishings with which we, as an Organization, outfit our bases is something I tried for years, with no success, to talk the Professor out of. "Do you have any idea," I said time and again, "of the price differential between custom and factory furniture?" But the Professor just waved a dismissive hand and ordered a half dozen more torturous stools from Nils Nykvist, famed Swedish designer of a style that's come to be known as "anticomfortable."

The leather chairs parked around the conference table are twelve in number, and each carries a price tag of twenty-five thousand dollars. With my arrival, nine were filled. The chair opposite me, at the far end of the table, would soon hold the Professor. The other two would remain vacant, as their usual occupants, Jerry and Terry Parker, twin demolition experts from the wilds of southeastern Arkansas, brothers rumored to have been raised by razorbacks, were out on assignment. "Have we heard from the twins?" I said.

Not far from the table, Rags Randall perched on a high stool in the bend of a U-shaped desk. In response to my query he began clicking keys, and eight colossal flat-screen monitors mounted on the walls of the octagonal room blinked to life. Each screen held an image of Jerry and Terry. The twins wore rappelling gear and stood near the edge of what appeared to be a rock cliff. Behind them, hundreds of small, uniformly shaped pink cylinders had been stacked into a neat pile.

"Dynamite," I said, nodding at Rags in approval. "Excellent work."

Rags never speaks—whether this is a matter of *can't* or *won't* doesn't seem to matter—and whenever we stand next to each other, he takes my hand. The boy's brown eyes are enormous, dark-ringed, and disturbingly soulful. His small hand is always sticky, and though my instinct is to pull away from his touch, I don't. I can recall taking your hand the same way as a boy, thousands of times, and I remember the images that would orbit through my mind as I clung to you—Rocky Mountains and giant sequoias and El Capitan, a granite monolith in Yosemite National Park—things deeply embedded, enduring, solid. I cannot help but feel saddened by the thought of what Rags must see as he clings to me.

On the monitors we watched Jerry Parker, or perhaps it was Terry Parker, clench his fists at his sides. He announced that he was ready, and he closed his eyes. His twin brother then punched him square in the testicles. Each of us seated around the table, Bea included, gasped aloud. As the twin who'd fallen, clutching his crotch, rose shakily and prepared to give his brother the same treatment, Rags used a joystick to pan out to a wide-angle shot. Jiang said something in Chinese. The rest of us turned to Bea for a translation.

"Fuckin' A," Bea said. "That's pretty goddamned majestic."

We nodded. Although the monument was something that we as an Organization would soon destroy, it was impossible to argue with its majesty.

"Forefathers!" The Professor had entered the Control Room, and he shuffled toward one of the flat screens as fast as his feet would allow. "Bastards!" he cried. In front of the monitor, the old man slapped feebly at the images of four American presidents. I rose, crossed to the Professor, took his shoulders, steered him toward his chair.

"I can see having something against Jefferson, Roosevelt, even Washington," said Bea, "but what could you have against Lincoln, Professor? He put down a civil war. He freed the slaves."

The Professor nodded. "He wanted to play daddy to the niggers, too."

The Control Room grew uncomfortably still. Even a year earlier, anyone who'd dared to use a racial epithet in the Professor's presence would have been shot in the face. The Professor is one-quarter Native American—Oglala Lakota to be precise—

and he's never tolerated bigotry. In fact, he integrated our Organization before blacks were allowed to sit at lunch counters or drink from public fountains in the southern U.S. One afternoon in Dr. Saleh's office, when the Professor referred to the neurologist as a "sand monkey," I explained all this, and the doctor said the disease tends to remove a patient's filters—that latent feelings, notions instilled in the patient at an impressionable age, can float to the forefront.

Inside Mount Overlord, I studied the hardened faces of our operatives. None of my assembled comrades blinked, nor did they give any indication of surprise or outrage at the Professor's out-of-character pronouncement. It's true that every member of our Organization has a great poker face and that as a group professional criminals are tough to offend. But I honestly felt, as I looked around the room, that no matter where our outlaw patriarch led, these people would follow. That their allegiance could be attributed to an impulse more lofty than greed, jealousy, or fear—those that tend to motivate us.

"And remember," said the Professor, glowering at us from beneath woolly old-man eyebrows, "that killing his father is the sworn duty of every son."

For the briefest of instants, the earth seemed to shift beneath our feet. We shot curious glances at one another as, on the monitors, the images of Jerry and Terry Parker dissolved and were replaced by eight sets of one hundred individual boxes. Each box contained a close-angle shot of a person's head. A few of the heads belonged to women, but most were men sporting similar haircuts, shirt collars, and neckties. Pressed to the right temple of each of these heads was the business end of an automatic weapon.

"Brilliant," said Bea. The rest of our assembly grinned in agreement. It felt like old times.

"Ladies and gentlemen," I said, rising, setting out to circumnavigate the conference table, "I'd like to thank each of you for joining us this morning, for agreeing to take part in our powwow."

On the screens, a hundred sets of terrorized eyes testified to how little choice the heads that contained them had had in the matter.

"I'm sure each of you," I continued, "must be wondering what is going on. Who has taken you hostage. What they want. How they managed to get past your heavily armed crackerjack security teams without alerting a soul."

In the upper right-hand corners of the screens, a scuffle broke out as one of the heads attempted to free itself and was rewarded with a machine-gun butt to the temple. Afterward, the head sat bleeding and sobbing, softly.

"Resistance is futile," I said. "However, it isn't our Organization's intent to harm any of you. We're simply interested in striking a bargain. Setting up a symbiotic situation. In short, we have a proposition. Would you like to hear it?"

Haltingly, inside their boxes, a handful of the heads nodded.

I looked at Rags, who clicked his keyboard, causing each of the monitors to divide into halves. On the left were the boxes containing the one hundred heads. On the right were Jerry and Terry Parker, kneeling on either side of their piled explosives, all four arms extended in a manner that suggested game show hostesses or magician's assistants. "Unless our demands are met," I said, as Rags panned out, "by five o'clock p.m. today, Coordinated Universal Time, our Organization will obliterate this singular and most majestic of American monuments."

Shocked stuttering broke out among the heads. The prodding of gun barrels silenced the sounds.

"Our demands," I continued, "are simple. You people run the most powerful nations on the planet, and all we ask, in exchange for the preservation of this seminal American landmark, is that each of you resigns his or her post. Effective immediately."

This time the shocked stuttering was not so easy to silence. Additionally, there was a significant amount of snorting and scoffing. The phrases "deranged madmen," "criminally insane," "nonsensical ravings," and "lunatic mind" could be distinguished and were uttered repeatedly. Many of the heads had to be slapped in the mouth.

"Each of you," I said, "will write a formal letter of resignation. You'll deliver one copy to your congress, parliament, ministry, or cabinet and the other copy to an address that will be provided. If just one of you fails to deliver these letters, a certain mountain in the Black Hills of South Dakota will be blown sky-high at precisely five oh one p.m. today."

A bald head whose box was located in the lower left-hand corners of the flat screens cautiously lifted a hand.

"Yes?" I said.

"Why?" he said.

By this time, I'd traveled around the marble-topped conference table, and I stood to the Professor's left. I was preparing to answer the bald head when a throat cleared itself beside me, when I felt a hand on my elbow. The Professor was rising to his feet, and though there's really no resemblance between you, I swear that for a moment it was you I saw standing there. You stood how you stood on every Thanksgiving of my childhood, patiently waiting for those of us gathered around the table at Grandma Jean's to quiet down, to bow our heads. Or no, you stood as I found you in the darkened kitchen, not long after my first encounter with the Professor. I arrived home in the small hours, dog-tired from my violent and illegal nocturnal labors, dying for a taste of Mom's leftover pot roast. I opened the refrigerator and, in its dim light, caught sight of you standing in front of a blank wall, staring straight ahead like a catatonic. You reminded me of a slab of concrete or a hunk of granite. You held up two of the stolen purses I'd buried in my bedroom closet. *I love you, Carl,* you said, *but I can't allow a hoodlum to keep working at the office. What am I going to do with you?* I let the refrigerator door swing closed, dousing the two of us in darkness. I stalked down the hall to my bedroom, threw a few things in a duffel, and fled the house where I grew up, never to return.

"I have no children," said the Professor, his gaze roaming from the hundred heads on the monitors to the faces of the nine underlings gathered in his Central Control Room, "other than those I've stolen from others. Still, over the years I've learned a thing or two about being a father. The hardest part of the job is taking off the training wheels, watching nestlings attempt to fly, watching them fall, watching them hurt themselves again and again. The temptation is to rush in, pick them up, correct for errors, make everything all right, but that's never the way to proceed. What a father must learn to do is step aside. Turn his back. Lay down his life. For it is only in the usurping of his progenitor that any of us becomes an adult. If you think of your nations as your children, then it is your duty—your obligation—to let them go. Let them make their own mistakes. Live their own lives."

Just then, the floor of the Control Room pitched unmistakably, drunkenly. My comrades all sat bolt upright. Ominous sounds emanated from miles beneath our feet. Groanings, rumblings, crackings. Into my mind tumbled a fantastic image, of a family of giants living deep inside Mount Overlord. It sounded as though these giants had just arisen from a nap, one that had lasted seven million years, as though they were now wrestling and arguing and making love and snapping redwoods over their knees to use as kindling. I glanced at Jiang, and in his startled eyes I spied corroboration. He said something in Chinese. The rest of us turned to Bea.

"Mount Saint Helens," Bea said. "Mount Saint Helens!"

Understanding bloomed across the battle-scarred faces that ringed the table, and a solitary scream pierced the air. A couple of my comrades bolted from the room, leaving an eye patch and a peg leg in their wake.

"No." The bald head was still speaking from the lower left corners of the eight monitors. His hand was still raised. "That's not what I meant. I wasn't asking why you want us to resign our posts but why you're bothering to make such a futile demand in the first place."

"Futile?" said the Professor.

"Yes," said the head. "As in pointless. Empty. I mean, you can't really expect that all of us will comply. Actually, I don't think you can expect that *any* of us will comply. Not even the U.S. president. The loss of a single national monument cannot be weighed against the danger of the entire world being plunged, at the same moment, into a state of ungoverned chaos."

The Professor turned to me. I grasped his shoulder, which felt brittle, as though, if I squeezed too tightly, it would crumble.

"So I'm guessing," said the bald head, "that this is strictly about destruction. That for some reason you people are dying to watch Mount Rushmore explode."

You have no way of knowing this, but over the years I've kept in touch with Mom. Letters, Christmas cards. These illicit communiqués I've been forced to hide from the Professor, who insists that all members of his Organization renounce any allegiance to their biological families, that they permanently cut that cord and swear fidelity instead to him, the patriarch of our outlaw family. A couple years ago, in the post office box I maintain under a false name, there appeared a letter from

Mom. She insisted on seeing me, and eventually I relented. We met in a chain coffee shop in a strip mall, miles from nowhere, and when I saw her seamed face, her shrunken frame, her wispy white hair, I broke down. She held me as I wept; we then ordered soy lattes. We sat in a corner so I could keep an eye out for moles and governmental agents, and she told me about your condition. The early-stage symptoms she described sounded exactly like what I'd been observing in the Professor.

"About six months ago," she said, "it became clear that I could no longer care for your father, and I was forced to move him into a facility. He doesn't know me, Carl, but every day he asks about you. When you're coming home. He worries about your room not being ready. About you not having enough money to pay for a flight. About whether the roads will be passable." Mom reached across the table and placed her hand, still delicate but now corded with veins, into my upturned palm. Her skin was cool and dry. When she pulled away, I saw that she'd left behind a tiny square of paper. We both stared down at this scrap. She didn't have to tell me what was written on it, or what she wanted me to do. "Please," she said softly, a devastating catch in her voice. "Please, Carl."

Standing beside the conference table in Mount Overlord's Control Room, which was now beginning to shudder and quake with increasing regularity, I gripped the Professor's shoulder. "Sometimes," I said to him, and to my comrades, and to the one hundred heads on the monitors, including the bald head in the lower left corners, "the only way to save something is to destroy it."

This wasn't an original thought. It was what the Professor said to me the morning after he fed Mort and Veronica to his albino alligators. Ever since, the two of us have been behaving as though the Professor was grooming me to take his place, to step into his colossal shoes, but this has never been the case. The truth is that when the Professor happened upon me twenty-five years ago, alternately assaulting and apologizing to that old drunk, he understood what you understood: that I possessed a certain resolve but that I lacked the stomach to execute my own resolutions. Unlike you, however, the Professor knew precisely what to do with me. He installed me in my current position only because he was convinced that I would never pose a threat to his authority, and for all intents and purposes he was right. After all, when Mom gave me the name and address of your assisted living facility that day in the coffee shop, when she essentially asked me to put you out of your misery, I couldn't do it. I traveled to the facility, peered into your room through the window, saw you lying on the twin bed, a papery, dusty shell of your former self. But I couldn't bring myself to go inside, to stand next to your bed. I couldn't bring myself to take your hand.

Though I never shared this story with the Professor, he knew that these events transpired. As he always already knew everything about me. About all his operatives. In painting me a false picture of my future in our Organization, he was merely protecting his interests, following his instincts. And though he recognized the possibility of betrayal from without, the Professor never imagined the possibility of betrayal from within. That his own brilliant mind could turn on him never made it onto his radar. Still, and in spite of everything, if I had my life to live over, I would elect to spend it serving the Professor. I've learned so much about the management of human beings, the commitment of global crimes, the implementation of diabolical schemes. In fact, it was my idea to relocate our headquarters. To place us all inside this volcano.

And now the eruption of Mount Overlord is making it impossible to move around our Antarctic base of operations. Electronic equipment and crockery and toiletries are shimmying from shelves, shattering against floors, and my comrades are fleeing the stratovolcano. I try to force Rags to depart with Bea, but the boy refuses. Shaking his head, he drops to the floor, wraps his spindly arms around my thighs. I reach down, detangle him. Lower myself to one knee. For what seems an eternity, I gaze into his eyes—large, soulful brown mirrors. Then Rags is in my arms and I'm crushing him to me, burying my face in his hair, which smells of cotton and sunshine.

In a matter of moments, only Rags, the Professor, and I will remain inside Mount Overlord. The Control Room will grow unbearably warm, and we'll strip down to our underpants but will continue to sweat like bastards. We'll pull three of Nils Nykvist's absurdly expensive leather chairs across the octagonal room to the only flat-screen monitor left hanging. Rags will use his joystick to pan around and we'll watch Jerry and Terry Parker put the finishing touches on their explosive masterpiece. As the room roils, bounces, and spasms with increasing violence, we'll be forced to cling to our chairs or end up on the floor.

By 4:58 p.m., the twins will have rappelled to the bottom of the granite monument and will be crouched some distance away, waiting for our sign. We won't receive a letter of resignation from a single head of state, but this will come as no surprise. Seated between Rags and the Professor, I will take one of each of their hands and weep, perhaps with sorrow, perhaps with fear, perhaps because the superheated, noxious fumes bubbling up beneath me will start to scramble my brain. When the Professor asks if it's lunchtime, I will tell him that I love him. When Rags says he loves me, I will tell him that I love him, too. When I nod at the boy, Rags will depress a button on his joystick. Collectively we'll marvel at what the remaining flat-screen monitor shows us: ancient granite dissolving into gray plumes, into jets of dark dust that rocket straight up and float idly in too-blue South Dakota skies before raining back down to earth. And this will make me think of you. Of what I hope you can no longer remember. Of what I pray you never forget.

Dear Delores Dale

I represent the estate of one Walter K. Brennan, owner of a popular Midwestern chain of fast-food eateries. Twelve days ago, Mr. Brennan lost a brief but grueling battle with esophageal cancer, and I have now disposed of his assets as instructed, with the exception of a single item—an item he bequeathed to you.

I know you never met Walter Brennan, Mrs. Dale, and are probably wondering what I am playing at. If I am some psycho merely masquerading as an attorney. Let me assure you, nothing could be further from the truth . . . though at times I think I might prefer institutional life to shaking hands and arguing cases, to sitting in snarled traffic and sighing and making occasional love to my dear wife.

Walter Brennan saw you only once, at a Dairy Queen fifty-eight years ago, and in his words, you "stole his heart." So that is what he left you.

Obviously I cannot excise Mr. Brennan's heart, cure it, and ship it to you. I was his attorney for sixteen years, but I never saw the man cry or even smile until the morning he sat across from me describing your lips as they curled around the stripy straw through which you drank a vanilla milk shake six decades ago. On that morning, Mr. Brennan broke down, sobbed so hard I was forced to lend him my favorite handkerchief.

And last night, when I asked my dear wife how on earth to

honor Walter K. Brennan's strange bequest, she smiled sagely and asked me one question.

What did you do with that handkerchief?

Please forgive the state of my handwriting, Mrs. Dale. I have never before composed a piece of correspondence upon a hankie.

Yours Most Sincerely,
Paul Wainscot, Attorney-at-Law

Mannequin and Wife

Steve showed up a week after the break-in. Dressed as a sailor. Wide white trousers, blue knotted neckerchief, flappy collar, jaunty white cap. Dan and Lila had just breakfasted and were settling into the living room with the Sunday *Times* when they spied him on the lawn, gleaming against the spring green, peering in at them through the picture window.

"Dan," said Lila, from a corner of the sofa, "is that seaman giving us the finger?"

"I believe," said Dan, from the desk, "that's a salute."

Ten minutes later, when they'd tired of arguing over the sailor's hand gesture, they stepped into slippers, pulled on robes, and ventured out to investigate. Leaving the safety of the flagstone path that snaked through the lawn from front door to curb felt, to the couple, like diving into the deep mystery of the ocean.

"You win," said Lila when they stood in the grass on either side of the mannequin. "It's a salute."

Dan tented a hand over his eyes, peered down Pembroke Drive in one direction and then the other. All he saw on this sleepy morning were brick ranches and bungalows with bright lawns, a neighborhood that at times felt more like a film set than an honest-to-God place. "Where do you suppose it came from?"

Lila touched the sailor's sleeve, rubbed the dense fabric between thumb and forefinger. "No idea."

"What should we do with it?"

"Bring it inside."

Dan studied his wife. "You want to bring it in the house?"

"I do." Lila seized one of the sailor's arms and indicated that her husband should do the same. "Quickly."

"But Lila." Dan grasped the other arm. "He doesn't belong to us."

"He's on our lawn. And possession is nine-tenths of the law."

Steve was far lighter than he looked. Lighter than seemed possible. *Shiver me timbers,* Dan thought, as he and Lila spirited the dummy inside.

Neither of them had ever before manipulated a mannequin, and they had fun with Steve. They took to setting the sailor up in various locales around the house—with them at the table as they dined or beside them on the couch, evenings, as they watched television. Once, Dan sat Steve on the commode, white pants around his ankles, and stuck the newspaper in his hands. Another time he set him up in the bathroom while Lila was showering, a warm towel draped over his arms. And a week after Steve arrived, on the morning Dan was to return to work for the first time since the break-in, Lila positioned the sailor before the stove and tied an apron around him, so that Steve appeared to be cooking Dan's eggs.

"Over medium, my good man," Dan said, seating himself at the Formica table.

"I'm afraid the navy," Lila said, as she delivered Dan's plate and settled opposite him, "only taught him scrambled."

Dan watched his wife salt and pepper her food. "You all right?"

She shrugged. “Decent. OK. Not fantastic.”

“I don’t have to go,” Dan said. “I can call Beckman. Take another week.”

“You’ve got to go sometime. What difference would another week make?”

“I don’t know.”

“And Steve’s here now,” Lila said. “He’ll keep me company.”

Dan turned and found that the sailor was seated at the table between them, rubbing his rigid hands together as he contemplated a steaming plate of eggs and toast.

“How long has he been there?” Dan said.

Lila shook her head. “What?”

“How did Steve get to the table?”

“What do you mean?”

“Did you put him in that chair?”

Lila glanced at the dummy’s blue neckerchief and saw herself at eight, hiding behind a black oak on a summer afternoon, watching her grandfather, a retired rear admiral, teach her brother how to tie a square knot. “Of course.”

Dan shook his head. “I missed it.”

“Sweetheart,” she said, “you weren’t looking.”

Returning to work was a relief for Dan. He loved sitting for hours on a lab stool, his right eye pressed to a compound microscope, searching for signs of genetic abnormality and mutation in samples collected by prison doctors across the tristate area. He’d just spotted a DNA sequence that indicated hyperthyroidism when Imogene spoke up.

“You poor things.” Though five years beyond retirement age, Imogene still worked three days a week at the station next to Dan’s. “I haven’t slept through the night since it happened.”

Their house had gone on the market not long after Dan started at the lab, and it was thanks in large part to Imogene, who lived two blocks from the couple, that their offer had been accepted. Theirs was a nice neighborhood—the sort of place where people still didn't bother to lock their doors.

"How's Lila?" Imogene asked.

"She'll survive."

"I'm buying a watchdog. Or a bouncer. Which would be a better investment?"

"Imogene. It was an isolated incident."

"What did they take?"

"Electronics, jewelry, silver. The usual."

"And you were home?"

Dan nodded.

"Sleeping?"

"At first."

Imogene looked up from her microscope, loosed the glass slide she'd been studying from the tiny metal arms that pinned it, and crossed to Dan's station. He slid the sliver beneath his lens, closed one eye, adjusted the scope, and whistled. "Shiver me timbers," he said.

"*Shiver me timbers?*"

"I'd hate to make this man's acquaintance in a dark alley."

"Dan." Imogene placed a knotty hand on his shoulder. Her white head bobbed as her timeworn face pressed close to his. "I believe you are in *crisis.*"

"Imogene."

"All right," she said. "But talking helps, my friend."

Two days later, Dan returned from work to find the house unnaturally still. Clutching briefcase and lunch bag, he stole from the front door on tiptoes, down the hall to the kitchen, where he found Steve slumped at the table, shirtless, his painted face hidden in his hands. Before the mannequin were the quart of bourbon Lila's father had gifted Dan the previous Christmas—mostly empty, and on its side, as though someone had been playing spin the bottle—a highball glass, and a photograph. Dan leaned over the dummy's shoulder and spied, within the photo's white borders, a female mannequin. She wore a sundress and sandals that laced up her calves; a blue cardigan hung from her shoulders. And though her hair was shorter and a different shade of brown, she bore a remarkable resemblance to Dan's wife.

"Lila?"

He found her in the studio—a converted sun parlor with three walls of glass. She was at work on a seascape she'd started the day before the break-in, her chin, cheeks, and forehead streaked with pigment. It was part of a series: large, nautical-themed oils, most of them dark and stormy. The scene Dan now contemplated on his wife's canvas was utterly still, and brightly lit. In the foreground was a three-masted schooner, in the distance an ocean liner illumed by the rising sun. In the lower right corner Lila had painted a small, battered dinghy. When Dan entered the room, she was outlining two human bodies a-bob in the swells, not far from the tiny vessel.

"Who's that?" he said.

She shook her head. "I'm not sure."

"What's with Steve?"

"He misses his wife."

"His wife?" he said. "The one in the picture?"

Lila nodded. She put down her brush. "I'm worried about him."

"Steve?" said Dan. "You're worried about the dummy?"

She nodded again. "I want to help him."

Dan thought of Rocky, an injured raccoon Lila had found not long after they wed. Once she'd nursed him back to health, Rocky followed Lila around like a puppy, but whenever Dan came near his wife, the animal attacked him. As he rubbed a scar Rocky's teeth had left on his forearm, a strange dread washed over Dan. "What can we do?"

"Find her."

"Who?"

"His wife. We can find Steve's wife."

Friday morning at the lab, Dan opened his briefcase to find Steve's wife staring up at him. He lifted the photograph and studied its subject—the mannequin that seemed to be Lila at a standstill. Lila fixed in space and time.

"Dan?"

Imogene stood at his shoulder, her cottony head bobbing.

"That's not your wife," she said.

"No," he said, "but she is *a* wife."

"Whose?"

"No one you know."

"Your friend," she said, "married a dummy?"

"It's complicated."

Imogene reached out, took the photo. "Shiver me timbers." She crossed the rubber matting that coated the lab floor—a surface designed to relieve tension and fatigue in the bodies of those who toiled upon it—opened a drawer in her desk, produced a magnifying glass nearly the diameter of her head, and examined the picture. "Dan," she said. "I *know* her."

"You do?"

She nodded. "I pass her all the time."

"Where?"

"Downtown."

He approached the old woman, gripped her quivering shoulders. "Show me?"

Four hours later, Dan and Imogene were strolling down Second Avenue eating hot dogs with mustard—a lunch purchased from a man wearing fingerless gloves, an overcoat, and a stocking cap despite the balmy, sun-soaked day.

"This is my favorite place," said Imogene, indicating the vast sheet glass windows they passed, one after another, "to ramble. And make believe."

They passed Fordham's and Grimmsby's, Havershire's and Bleinheim's, Southfort's and Frederickson's. In the window of Cohn's, they found Steve's wife.

"Oh, Dan," said Imogene. "The photo doesn't do her justice."

She stood in a sizeable bay surrounded by three walls of glass, wearing a sailor suit made for a woman: white knee-length dress, blue neckerchief, rounded collar, snappy white cap. Her left elbow rested on a wooden rail and her right hand was pressed to her forehead in a salute. Dan inspected Steve's wife from every angle; no matter where he stood, her painted blue eyes followed.

"She looks lonely," he said.

"She had a companion," said Imogene. "A male mannequin, also dressed in seafaring style. But then someone broke in."

"Broke in?"

"And stole her partner. Or at least I assume. One of the windows was broken, and it took Cohn's a couple of days to replace it."

Or perhaps, Dan thought, as he toed a shard of glass Cohn's had failed to clear from the sidewalk, *her partner broke out.*

That evening Dan discovered Steve and Lila in the living room, on the sofa. Or rather, Steve was on the sofa and Lila was seated on Steve's lap. Lila's eyes were closed, her right ear pressed to the sailor's painted mouth. It seemed to Dan that his wife's face was lit from below. By an invisible flashlight, wielded by an unseen hand.

"Lila?"

She leaped up. From across the room, Dan saw a tremor move through her limbs.

"Dan," she said, "this isn't what it looks like."

"It's not."

She shook her head.

"What is it?"

"Steve was just telling me," she said, "about Bess."

"Bess."

"His wife."

Dan circled the sofa until he had a clear view of Steve. The dummy sat motionless, shoulders slumped, head down. For the first time, Dan noticed that Steve's hair was thinning, and he thought, *Imogene is right. I* am *in crisis. Mannequins don't go bald.*

"He was telling me," Lila said, "about the first time he saw her."

"Was he?"

She nodded. "She wasn't even Bess yet. Just a torso and a head. No limbs, no hair, not even a painted face. He watched them put Bess together and drape her in a designer wedding gown. Raw silk, in muted ivory. And before Steve knew it, he and Bess were standing side by side in a display window, atop a plywood platform tiered like a cake."

"A whirlwind courtship," said Dan.

She smiled.

"I don't suppose Steve told you," Dan said, "why he left Bess? Standing alone in a window at Cohn's?"

Lila sat beside the rigid sailor. She touched Steve's knee, and Dan felt his hands clench into fists.

"Steve left his wife," she said, "because he couldn't save her."

After wandering suburban, then urban, streets for hours, Dan found himself back on Second Avenue, where projected ponds of light drowned out shadow and night. *Do all life's roads,* he thought, *lead to commerce?* As he stood before Cohn's, studying Steve's wife—serene smile, sharp salute—two men appeared within the glass display. After disassembling the smokestack that stood behind Bess and carting out the pieces, the pair crept up on the mannequin and seized her. Lifted her over their heads. As they unfastened hooks and eyes, undid buttons, unzipped zippers, stripped away dress and shoes and underclothes, Bess reached for the window with rigid hands. Her painted eyes pleaded with Dan, but he just stood there, rooted. Frozen.

"I'm sorry," he said. "I'm so goddamned sorry."

The window dressers left Bess on her side, naked. Exposed for all the world to see. Dan shifted his focus to the sheet of glass before him. He skimmed its surface in search of flaws—markers of abnormality—but found none. The pane was spotless, whole, unblemished, and Dan considered how much strength would be required to pass through it. Not to smash through with fists or a weapon but merely to step through the transparent barrier that separates outside from inside, real from make-believe, visible from microscopic, animate from inanimate, home from prison, husband from wife.

"Hang on, Bess," he told the fallen woman in the glass box. "Just hang on."

Dan found Lila and Steve at the kitchen table, gripping steaming mugs of herbal tea.

"Lila," Dan said, "we've got to get downtown."

"Downtown? It's nearly midnight."

"Midnight?" He started opening and closing drawers. "We'd better get a move on."

Lila rose to her feet. "What's this about?"

"Bess."

Lila glanced at Steve. Steve stared dead ahead. "Bess?"

"She's in trouble." Dan pulled out a flashlight. Shreds of the Morse code he'd learned as a Cub Scout drifted over his transom, and he tested the beam, flashing *S-O-S, S-O-S,* against the white of a kitchen wall. "Bess is in crisis."

"Crisis?"

Dan nodded. "She needs our help."

The couple turned to Steve and found that the sailor had abandoned his seat and now stood at the back door, one hand on the knob, a look of urgency and worry etched into his wooden face.

"Attaboy," Dan said. "But first we'll need to change."

Thirty minutes later, he parked their six-year-old sedan across the street and down the block from Cohn's. He wore black, as did Lila and Steve. Before climbing out of the car, Dan and Lila covered their faces, as well as Steve's, with worn stocking caps into which Lila had cut lopsided eyeholes.

"Ready?" Dan said.

"No," said Lila.

"No?"

"I don't get what we're doing."

"Reuniting Steve and Bess."

"How?"

"By breaking into Cohn's."

"Breaking in?" Lila shook her masked head. "Have you lost your mind?"

"Perhaps."

"We'll go to prison."

"I doubt that."

"Why?" She shook her head again. "Why are we doing this?"

For the first time since the break-in, Dan reached for his wife. He stroked the woolen material obscuring her left cheek. "We've got to see it."

"See what?"

He took a breath. "The other side."

And then they were sliding stealthily from the sedan. Extracting Steve from the backseat. Peering around for witnesses. Spiriting the mannequin across the street and over the sidewalk to Cohn's. For a full minute they stood in a row before the window—a black-clad, ski-masked trinity contemplating poor naked Bess, who lay where the window dressers had dropped her. When Dan and Lila turned to Steve, they found his cap yanked up and tears coursing down his cheeks. His wooden fists were pressed against the vast pane of glass above his head, as though the dummy were about to start pounding.

* * *

Seven miles away, Imogene watched King, her new Doberman pinscher, lift his leg against a blue spruce in Dan and Lila's front yard.

"Sorry, Dan," she said. "Apologies, Lila."

King dragged the old woman back to her bungalow. As the canine lapped water from a metal bowl in the kitchen, Imogene entered her laboratory. Her husband had passed on a year earlier, and she'd taken to bringing her work home. She settled on a tall stool and pressed her quivering head forward.

"What on earth?"

Before she left to walk King, Imogene had been studying the magnified blood of a career criminal—a recidivist whose crimes included breaking and entering, larceny, assault, and rape. But now she wondered if her microscope had mutated into a kaleidoscope. All she could make out were fragmented colors and shapes. Imogene pulled away from the scope, examined the slide, and discovered that the delicate glass pane was broken. Smashed into a dozen shards.

"Shiver me timbers."

Imogene called King, and together she and the dog crept through the house, searched every nook and corner, but found no trace of an intruder.

As they watched Steve step forward and pass through Cohn's display window without disturbing its transparent surface, Dan and Lila felt their limbs and joints stiffen, felt their soft parts grow rigid and still, and it seemed to the couple that the glass before them wasn't a window but a canvas, or a screen. And they were watching not Steve and Bess but a moving picture of themselves, saying things that needed to be said. An impossible film, made without their knowledge or consent.

"I should have saved you," said the husband.

"Stop it," said the wife.

"I should have."

"You couldn't have."

"Why not?"

"We can't save each other."

"What can we do?"

"Forgive each other."

"You forgive me?"

"I do."

"I'll never forgive myself."

"I know."

"So what can I do?"

"Hold me."

"Now?"

"Always."

As the husband dropped to his knees and embraced his naked wife, it seemed to Dan and Lila as if the world were filling with water. In no time the couple was afloat, facing each other, their inflexible bodies knocking rhythmically together. They spied a dinghy in the distance, just big enough for two. And though they knew that eventually they would reach the boat and clamber inside, row themselves to shore and return to their shared home, as well as their separate lives, for the moment Dan and Lila were content to bob face-to-face, immersed in a unity that will elude the living until we learn to be utterly still.

Acknowledgments

I wish to thank the editors of the following literary journals, in which versions of these stories first appeared: *Atticus Review:* "We Can Learn from the Sawhorse"; *Barrelhouse:* "Sometimes, They Kill Each Other"; *Best Small Fictions 2020* and *Pidgeonholes*: "Dear Delores Dale"; *Blue Earth Review:* "Well-Built Men, 18 to 30, Who Would Like to Be Eaten by Me" and "Insight"; *Crazyhorse* and *Sequestrum:* "Come Back, Rita"; *Harpur Palate:* "Mannequin and Wife"; *The Iowa Review:* "Rebirth of the Big Top"; *Jellyfish Review:* "Breach"; *Joyland:* "Victoria"; *Mid-American Review:* "Burro"; *One Story:* "Mastermind"; *Salamander:* "Iphigenia in Baltimore"; *SFWP Quarterly:* "Options Counseling"; *The Southeast Review:* "Hobbled" and "Chrysalis"; *storySouth:* "Possible Wildlife in Road"; *Washington Square Review:* "By the Numbers."

I would also like to express my deep appreciation for my teachers, supporters, and friends, among them Tommy Hays, Heather Newton, Maggie Marshall and Steve Goldman, Cathy Hankla, Jeanne Larsen, Richard Dillard, Liz Poliner, Leah Stewart, Chris Bachelder, Jim Schiff, Michael Griffith (one of the most generous literary citizens I know), Beth Harris, Christine Harris, Catherine Miller, Maya Gorton, Rob Castillo, Morgan Griggs, Brittney Scott, Todd Lester, Sarah Anne Strickley and Ian Stansel, Stacey Atchison and Ian Moore, Kay Spencer, Yvonne Rodgers, Libbie Dougan, Katherine and Sam Terry, Elizabeth Spencer, Steve Spencer and family. And a very special thank you to my husband, Bill Gatewood.

I must also thank the woman who taught me everything

I know (which explains a lot): my mother, Julie Ann Terry Fawkes Johns. In my mind, forever dancing with a door in some crackerbox apartment, snapping loudly and singing off key. My first and most fervent supporter. I can still see her typing like the wind at a rickety card table, hammering out a novel—now sadly lost to time—titled *Savage Destiny*.

CPSIA information can be obtained
at www.ICGtesting.com
Printed in the USA
LVHW042232021120
670484LV00009B/2178